STILL
ANONYMOUS

Vincent L. Scarsella

**DIGITAL
CRIME
FICTION**

*Donna:
Happy Reading!
Thank you!
Vito L. Scarsella*

DIGITAL FICTION
PUBLISHING CORP

Part One
Lost

Chapter One
A Son

He's my son, Jerry Shaw thought as he stood before the glass partition of the infant nursery, staring down at the seven-pound, eleven-ounce pink-faced baby boy innocently sleeping in a crib near the center of the wide, bright room. It was mid-afternoon, and there was no one else present in the quiet hallway of the Celebration General Hospital maternity ward. On the other end of the hall were the rooms for the mothers who had just given birth to the infants now slumbering or crying in the nursery.

A nurse had printed the name of Jerry's newborn on a placard in front of his crib in bold, red letters: **Seius Shaw Martin.** The boy had taken the surname of his mother, Jade Martin. He had to. After all, an anonymous man could not claim a son.

The boy's name had come to Jerry while surfing the

internet late one night for names that described his birthright—
that he was the son of an anonymous man, John Doe, and the
invisible man rolled into one. Jerry had stumbled on the Latin
name, *Seius*, that meant essentially, a fictitious name under the
laws of ancient Rome. Perfect, he'd thought. Not John or
Nicholas or David for this boy, the son of the Anonymous
Man. It was to be Seius. After some pleading, Jade had
reluctantly agreed to it but only if the child also could take as
his middle name Jerry's name—Shaw.

Jerry wore a navy-blue hoodie with the hood pulled up over
his head, thus hiding his face and eyes, as he hunched forward
and stared down at his newborn son. That wasn't so strange,
even for central Florida, considering the temperature had
dropped over the last couple of days. By that mid-afternoon, it
had risen to only sixty-five. Chilly for late October in these
parts, but Jerry wore hoodies even on the hottest of days.

Jerry finally pulled himself away from the glass and walked
down the hallway to the patients' room. Jade was in Room 407.
She'd given birth to Seius late the previous night and was still
pretty worn out from the experience. A night baby, just like his
Daddy, she'd happily told Jerry moments after she'd pushed the
child into the world. According to Jerry's birth certificate, he'd
had been born at 1:59 AM.

As Jerry walked into the room, Faith Smith, sitting on a
wide chair at the side of Jade's bed, lowered her iPad and put a
finger to her lips requesting Jerry's silence. Jade was asleep on
the propped-up bed. Jerry nodded, walked over and stood at
the bedside. Jade looked as beautiful as ever, though her face
and eyes were puffy from the ordeal of childbirth the previous
night.

After a time staring down at her, for some reason, Jerry

thought of his wife, Holly. The striking resemblance between Jade and Holly had continued to haunt Jerry all these months, and sometimes, even during the best of times with Jade, like now, he'd think of Holly. Like what Holly might have looked like asleep in a hospital bed up in Buffalo after giving birth to their imaginary son.

"You saw him?" whispered Faith and after Jerry nodded, she added, "Isn't he beautiful?"

Faith was Jade's best friend from her Binghamton escort service days. She'd been the only person Jade had kept in touch with, through occasional cell phone calls, after Jade had left Binghamton with Jerry to become his front with the world in the area around Disney World. Three months ago, Jade had permitted Faith to come down to Florida and live with them in order to change her life after hiding for a few weeks under the symbolic, invisible cloak of Jerry as The Anonymous Man.

Jerry turned to Faith with a wide smile and whispered, "Yes, he is." He sighed thinking of his son. "That's because he looks like her."

Despite his low voice, Jade stirred. She opened her eyes and turned to Jerry, and seeing him, smiled. As Jerry reached down and took her hand, Jade said, "He's got you in him, too."

Faith got up and told them she was going down to the cafeteria and asked if they wanted anything. Jerry gave her a ten-dollar bill for a coffee for himself and a ginger ale for Jade and off she went. After Faith left, Jerry laid down on the bed next to Jade.

"You alright?" he asked, drawing her close. as he drew her close.

She sighed and said, "Yeah. Sore. Tired. You must be tired, too."

9

Jerry yawned and closed his eyes.

"Don't get too comfy," Jade laughed. "Although, maybe you should take a nap because once I come home with our new bundle of joy, I'd don't think you'll be getting much sleep the next few weeks."

"He's worth it," Jerry said.

"I'll remind you you said that when he wakes you at three in the morning," she said.

Jerry yawned again and closed his eyes, and soon enough, he was gently snoring. Jade dozed off as well. Minutes later, a heavy-set nurse came in and apologized for having to wake them to take Jade's blood pressure. She was leaving the room as Faith returned. She handed Jerry his cup of coffee, and he sat on a chair next to the one she'd been occupying.

After a sip of the coffee, Jerry asked Faith if he could borrow her iPad. With a nod, she handed it to him, and he immediately opened *The Buffalo News* online site. He liked to check the goings on up north and hadn't yet done so that day after the long night. He scrolled down the highlighted national and local headlines until about half-way down, he saw a link to a story with the headline:

Shaw Murder Pair Out on Technicality

Tensing, Jerry immediately clicked the link to the story and read. As he did so, he stood. Jade was saying something about the baby to him, but he wasn't listening.

"Jerry? What?" she asked.

He looked up at her.

"What?"

"They—they got out," he said.

With a frown, she shook her head, not getting it.

"Who got out?"

"Them," he said. "Jeff, Holly."

Chapter Two
Jeff and Holly and Jerry and Jade

The following afternoon, Jade and Jerry brought the baby home. Jerry couldn't help but smile as he carried his son into their tan, four-bedroom stucco house in a gated residential development. Their secluded little burg called Davenport was in Northeast Polk County about fifteen minutes from Disney World. He and Jade tucked the baby into his crib in one of the smaller bedrooms that had been set up weeks ago as the nursery. Afterwards, they tip-toed out and plopped down into each other's arms on the couch in the living room. Faith was working as a waitress at a nearby Denny's, so they had the afternoon to themselves.

With her eyes closed, Jade asked, "So, you think they'll come after us."

Jerry sighed as he pulled her close. "What do you think? We have their money. Over a million dollars."

"It's not their money," Jade snapped.

"It's not our money either."

"They tried to steal it from you."

"Well, Jeff'll come and try and steal it again."

"Jeff, not Holly?" Jade asked. Jerry felt Jade tense in his arms. Her bringing Holly up was never a good thing. "You still doubt where her heart's been all this time?"

"Course not." Jerry sighed. He never liked going there. "My point is, they'll come after it. Jeff *and* Holly. They're a team. They know I have all that money and they want it. They'll try to find me—us."

Jerry accepted that Jade's concern about Holly was somewhat justified. That Jerry still had feelings for Holly, and would forever have such feelings, wasn't helped by his secretly bringing Holly down to Florida a year and half ago, in the midst of her first trial for his murder, and hiding her out from Jade in a cheap motel in Kissimmee for a week. Only another of Holly's betrayals of him—almost resulting in his murder by Jeff—had prevented the renewal of whatever relationship was left between them.

After Jade had rescued him from Jeff and Holly's murderous plot in that hotel room in Kissimmee, Jerry had tried to explain that he'd brought Holly down with him out of pity. She needed his help, and after all, they did have quite a long history, going back ten years. It was simply something that the Anonymous Man would do—enable her to change her life and become a new, better person while under his cloak.

, Jerry had added, "Like I said, Holly and I have history. Seven years of marriage and a couple years before that. She'd come along from out of nowhere back in college and propped me up at a time when I wasn't feeling so good about myself. I was fat and lowly and not going anywhere. She made me feel good about myself. For the first time in forever, I believed in myself.'" He had sighed as Jade glared at him, but he went on anyway. "What happened after a few years, I don't know. Why she stopped massaging my ego. Maybe it was my fault. I couldn't lose weight, couldn't feel better about myself, despite her cheerleading. I just started doubting myself again at some point, and that wasn't helped by not being able to get Holly pregnant.

"Anyway, at some point, we just started going through the motions of our marriage, our jobs. Then Jeff Flaherty came into our lives with the proposition that would change everything, that would enable each of us to escape our empty, humdrum lives."

Jade had reacted bitterly to this explanation. "And what have I done to massage your ego?" she asked. "Nothing?"

"You've done a lot, of course," Jerry replied. "Without you..."

"You still love her, don't you," she accused.

"No, of course not."

But Jade had turned away from him, and it was days before they talked meaningfully again. After that, he avoided discussing Holly. She became a festering wound in their otherwise strong relationship, the old lover never quite forgotten, who'd be brought up forever in times when Jade lost confidence in herself and doubted Jerry's love.

Over the months since then, Jerry had demonstrated to Jade that he loved her, and only her, and she seemed to accept that it was over between him and Holly. But in retrospect, that had been easy. After all, Holly had been in jail, unreachable. But today, all that had changed.

"How can they do that?" Jade asked him. "Find us?"

Jerry shrugged and said, "I have no idea. But everyone leaves a trail."

"Even a dead man? Even the Anonymous Man?"

Again, Jerry shrugged and looked away with his lips pressed tight. He was clearly troubled. He had too much on his plate— the baby, Jade, Faith, and now this to complicate and magnify everything else.

Finally, he turned to Jade and said, "Yes, even the Anonymous Man. They know we're down here, for one thing." After a sigh, a thought came to him. After another moment, he said, "Maybe I should call Jack Fox."

Jade knew all about Jack Fox, the former investigator from Global Life and Casualty who, for some unfathomable reason, had let Jerry go free in the cemetery up in Buffalo when, on his birthday in late September over a year ago, Jerry was foolishly compelled to go look at his name on the family gravestone. Some weeks after that, Jerry had sent issue number one of his superhero comic book, "The Anonymous Man" to Fox.

"Call him? Why?"

"Ask him to follow them around for a few days. See what they're up to. See if they intend to come after us."

"Think he'd do that? Isn't he retired?"

"I don't know. Who else can I ask? A dead man doesn't have many friends."

Jade sighed and leaned close to Jerry. "How'd they get out?" she asked. "You said on a technicality. What was it?"

"The paper said something about speedy trial," Jerry said. "The prosecutor screwed up somehow, didn't do what he needed to do to stop the prosecution clock. I don't quite understand it myself. All I know is that they're out, and there's no way for them to be tried again. They got off scot-free."

"So, they got away with murder?"

"Well, not exactly," Jerry said. "I'm not really dead."

"You know what I mean."

"I know," Jerry said. "They got away with Willie Robinson's murder."

Jade nodded. Jerry had told her all about Willie Robinson, who he and Holly and Jeff had called "the body guy." He was an anatomical preparator at the University of Buffalo Medical School who'd provided them the cadaver used as the substitute for Jerry's body in faking his death. Jeff had killed Willie Robinson because he'd demanded more money once he realized they'd gotten $4 million from Global Insurance.

In the next moment, they heard the baby wailing from the nursery. Parenthood kicked in. With a sigh, Jade pushed herself off the couch and went to him. A moment later, Jerry got up and followed after her.

Chapter Three
The Anonymous Man: Issues #1 and #2

Jade and Jerry were back on the couch an hour later after Seius had been fed and put down again. They promptly fell asleep in each other's arms. Twenty minutes later, Jerry woke and Jade soon followed. They yawned and stretched and sat up.

Through another yawn, Jade said, "Faith told me she'll be leaving soon."

"Is she sure?"

"That asshole, Julio's stopped coming around her mother's place looking for her," Jade explained. "Looks like he's given up finding her, moved on to other things, other girls. She's ready to be on her own. Also, we have the baby. She feels she's intruding."

"Whatever she wants to do," Jerry said. "As long as she feels safe, ready."

"She'll be fine on her own," Jade said and smiled. "She's

tired of hiding under the Anonymous Man's invisibility cloak."

"Well, that's what the Anonymous Man does," Jerry replied. "Gives a person a way to escape their troubled life and start a new one. He's their door to freedom."

Jade nodded and said, "Speaking of the Anonymous Man, where are you on the second Issue?"

"Almost finished," he said. "Needs some tweaking, some fine tuning."

"You gonna ever tell me what it's about?"

Jerry had been working on the story and illustrations for the superhero comic on-and-off the last few months. He spent long hours in the fourth bedroom at the front of the house that served as his office. A drawing table and high stool took up one corner of the room where he sat penciling his storyboards and jotting notes. Finally, after more than a year, he'd ink-sketched a near-final version of the second Issue of "The Anonymous Man" in his long drawing pad. But he had not yet shown it to Jade or even told her what the story was about.

"It continues from the end of the first issue," Jerry said.

Jade recalled that in Issue #1, the unnamed hero of the comic had escaped death in the South Tower of the World Trade Center on 9/11 because he'd been late for work at his investment firm after arguing about money with his wife that morning. It was this same money problem that had caused him to siphon funds from several client accounts to an offshore bank in the name of a limited liability company formed in New Mexico that allowed the owner to remain anonymous. Only the day before, on September 10th, an investigator from the SEC had contacted him at work and made an appointment for Wednesday of that week, September 12th, to review certain irregularities involving his clients' accounts.

When the hero arrived in lower Manhattan that morning, the planes had already struck the towers. By the time the North Tower collapsed, at 10:28, he was retreating from the dust, destruction, and death with hundreds of other scared New Yorkers to the George Washington bridge. Walking across the bridge amid the chaos and fear, the idea struck him—how to escape his money and legal problems and a disintegrating, childless marriage. He'd disappear. His wife and parents and sister and friends would think he'd been killed in his tiny cubicle on the 93rd floor with thousands of others who'd been vaporized when they went down with the tower during its surreal, fiery collapse into a mound of twisted wreckage and white ash. He'd become an anonymous man and start a new life.

Issue #1 skipped six months into the future, when its hero, the now Anonymous Man, had settled in Endicott, New York, next to Binghamton, living on the hundreds of thousands of dollars in the offshore account that the SEC wasn't looking for any longer. Its interest in that money, and him, had ended with his supposed death on 9/11.

Then, one warm summer night, while taking one of his usual solitary strolls around the neighborhood near his hulking old house, a woman around his age ran from the other direction straight into his arms. Her name, he soon learned, was Karen Smith. She was crying and trembling, fleeing from danger. That danger was her husband, Dan, a brutish man who had spent their five years of marriage physically and emotionally abusing her. The Anonymous Man led Karen back to his house and they stood in the shadows of the front stoop as Dan Smith ran past, stopping every now and then, pleading, admonishing, threatening and, like Stanley Kowalski in *A Streetcar Named*

Desire, shouting out Karen's name, begging her to take him back.

But Dan Smith wouldn't find Karen that night, or any other night after that, because she was hiding under the cloak of the Anonymous Man's anonymity; and, after several weeks, she'd emerge from that cloak into a new and better life. That was the Anonymous Man's "superpower." The ability to hide a person and help him or her escape a bad life and eventually emerge into and begin a new and better one.

"Yes, I know, from the end of issue number one," Jade said, and she paused a moment before continuing, "when that investigator, Oscar Plato, is hired by his sister, to find him."

As Issue #1 showed, the Anonymous Man's sister thought she had seen him running away from the collapsing buildings down some nameless Manhattan street, filmed by one of the many amateur cell phone videos made that morning. He was covered with soot and dust, escaping the destruction with hundreds of others and, therefore, extremely difficult to identify. Still, based upon this fleeting image, his sister became obsessed with the idea that he was still alive and for some reason, was hiding from his family and friends. So, she hired Oscar Plato, a private investigator, to find him.

"Yes, Issue two continues from the point when Plato is hired."

"Can you show it to me?" she asked. "What you have so far."

"It's not finished."

"Please?"

He sighed, ever fearful of showing his work to anyone, even her. Fearful of rejection. After a time, Jerry nodded and told her he'd get it for her. Moments later, he returned and, as he sat on the couch next to Jade, he handed her a large drawing pad with inked sketches of the various storyboard scenes. Jade started flipping through the pad, her eyes occasionally widening as the story unfolded, board by board. She finally reached the end and looked up at him.

"Well?"

After a moment, she smiled and said, "It's wonderful. A bestseller."

He shrugged doubtfully and said, "We'll see."

"I love it," Jade said. "It's great how you twist it around, so Dan Smith hires Oscar Plato to find his wife, Karen Smith, after Plato has given up finding him for the sister. The best is when Plato sits with the Anonymous Man in the diner and asks about Karen. Brilliant."

His smile broadened and, with a nod, he said, "I enjoyed drawing that scene."

She put down the pad and leaned close to him. "You're really talented, you know that Jerry. So now what? What're you gonna do with it? What's the next step?"

"I polish it, smooth off the rough edges. Then I'm gonna self-publish it on Amazon, along with Issue number one. It's easy enough to do."

"As Anonymous, right?" she asked.

He smiled. "Of course. That's who I am."

Chapter Four
Jack Fox

It had been over a year since Jerry had last seen Jack Fox at his fake gravestone in Holy Cross Cemetery. An urn in the grave contained the ashes of the poor guy who thought he'd donated his body to the University of Buffalo medical school. Instead, it had become part of the $4 million life insurance fraud scheme executed almost to perfection more than two years ago by Jerry, Holly, and Jeff. This perfect crime had been ruined by betrayal and greed on the part of Holly and Jeff. Now, for Jerry, the scheme had taken another ominous and unexpected turn.

Surfing the internet, Jerry quickly found Jack Fox's home address. What surprised him was that after retiring from Global Life & Casualty Insurance's Special Frauds Unit, Fox had moved from Philadelphia to Buffalo. Apparently, his time spent in Western New York hounding Holly and Jeff, and later, him, on Global's behalf, had sparked a fondness for the area. It was a lot less populated, crime-ridden, and expensive than Philly. Still, it seemed odd to retire to Buffalo. Like most northerners, Buffalonians retired far away from that cold, rustbelt city to warm, sunny climes like Florida and Arizona.

From a further search on the internet, Jerry obtained a cell phone number for Fox. Using the latest of the prepaid cell phones he bought for cash at various discount department stores every other month or so, Jerry dialed the number.

After the fourth ring, Fox answered with a tired, "Hello?" When Jerry hesitated a moment, Fox repeated, "Hello?"

"Ah, hello, Mister Fox?"

When Jerry again paused before getting into the purpose for the call, Fox sighed and said, "Yes. Help you?"

"Ah, yeah." Jerry sighed, and blurted, "It's, it's me, the Anonymous Man."

"Who?"

"You know," Jerry went on, "the guy in the cemetery. I sent you a comic book. 'The Anonymous Man.'"

That stopped Fox cold. A few weeks after the meeting at his fake gravestone, Jerry had sent Fox a self-published edition of Issue #1 of The Anonymous Man.

After a time, Fox let out a breath, a kind of chuckle, and said, "Oh, yeah."

Jerry had never completely understood why Fox had let him go that sunny afternoon in September over a year ago. Maybe the old investigator had come to admire Jerry's grit and resolve. He'd not only faked his death and successfully pulled off a major fraud worth $4 million, but he'd revenged the murderous betrayal of his wife and best friend. Catching Jerry in the cemetery on his birthday, staring at his fake grave, perhaps had been enough satisfaction for Fox. What was to be gained by sending Jerry to jail and getting Global back their money? Fox had left Global by then, and they had more than enough money. The $4 million they'd lost was a drop in the bucket, and anyway, Jeff Flaherty had given half of it back in exchange for a reduction of his sentence. Not to mention that Fox knew he'd be unable to outrun Jerry that warm September afternoon.

"What do you want, Mister Shaw?"

"I need a favor."

Fox laughed and said, "A favor? I already gave you one, a big one."

"Well, I need another."

Fox sighed. He suddenly realized what this call was about. "Oh, so you know they got out," he said. "Jeff and Holly. Travesty of justice."

"Yes, I know," Jerry said. "And yes, a travesty of justice. Now that they're out, for obvious reasons, I'm concerned for the safety of myself, the woman I love, and my newborn child."

"Newborn child? When?"

"Couple days ago."

"Boy, girl?"

"Boy."

"Healthy?"

"Yes."

"And the mother. Is she okay?"

"Doing fine."

"Same woman you brought down to Florida from Binghamton?"

"Yes, same woman."

"Good for you," Fox said. After a time, he added, "So, you're concerned because they got out. What does that have to do with me?"

"You're an investigator, right?"

"Yes, so? I'm retired," Fox said. He didn't find it necessary to add that on rare occasions he took a job following a suspected cheating spouse or a malingerer improperly drawing disability benefits.

"I know," Jerry said. He sighed, and blurted it out, "I was hoping I could hire you to follow them around for a few days— Holly and Jeff. See what they're up to."

"Up to no good, no doubt," Fox said, "if I know those two." Fox thought for a while.

After half a minute passed, Jerry said, "Mister Fox?"

"Yeah, sure," Fox finally answered. "I'll follow them for you."

"How much?"

"We'll figure that out later," Fox said. "See how much work it ends up being, what it costs me."

"Alright, that's fair," Jerry said. "And thank you, again."

"You're welcome," Fox said, "How can I reach you?"

"This number," Jerry said. "Should be on your phone. It's pre-paid."

Fox checked the screen of his phone, saw the number. "Got it," he said. "I'll try and call you every night, give you a regular report. Around eleven most evenings, okay?"

"Yes, perfect" Jerry said. "That'll work. And thanks again, Mister Fox."

"As I said, you're welcome," Fox said. After a sigh, he said, "I just have to ask you one thing, Mister Shaw."

"Yeah, what's that?"

"When's Issue number two coming out?"

Chapter Five
Stakeout

After forty-five years as an investigator, Jack Fox was used to long, tedious stakeouts. That was a necessary, though unpleasant, part of the profession—sitting for hours on end in the cramped discomfort of a car or van, without decent food, good air or an adequate means of relieving oneself.

Fox had been sitting for the last hour or so, since eight that morning, in his discreet, cramped Ford Focus on Colton Avenue in Lackawanna, New York, a dreary burg just south of Buffalo, a few houses down from an old clapboard house where Jeff Flaherty and Holly Shaw presently occupied the small, two-bedroom upper flat. During the wait, Fox had already read through *The Buffalo News* and finished the first chapter of *Lawyers Gone Bad,* a novel by a local author, on his iPad.

This was the second day he'd surveilled Holly and Jeff, and Fox hoped today would be more fruitful. Not that he wanted them to go chasing after his client to get their perceived share of the remaining one million or so of Global insurance money they'd stolen still in Jerry's possession. Rather, he was hoping that they'd do the opposite, find jobs and settle down together, get on with their lives. But he knew, as did Jerry Shaw, that was unlikely. It was almost a given that sooner rather than later, they'd come after Jerry and his ill-gotten money.

Late yesterday morning, they'd taken a taxi to a Sav-A-Lot, a discount supermarket. They'd come out with several boxes of groceries and returned to the apartment in another cab. It was a gray, drizzly, chilly day in late October and for the rest of that day, they'd stayed in, doing whatever in the upper flat: plotting, screwing, watching TV, boozing or searching the internet.

Around nine that second morning, Fox's interest perked when he saw Holly's younger brother, Raymond, pull into a spot not far from where Fox was parked. He watched as Raymond exited his car and walked down the driveway to the back entrance of Jeff and Holly's upper unit. From an online search of the city assessor's records, Fox already knew that Raymond owned the old double house, valued at just shy of $65,000. It was that tidbit of information that had led him to watch the house in the first place. He had smiled and whispered, "Bingo!" to himself the previous morning when he'd seen Jeff and Holly emerge from the back of the place and enter the cab on their way to the grocery store. Raymond was likely letting them stay in the small flat rent-free until they got on their feet; or, perhaps, he had joined their conspiracy to retrieve the million-plus dollars from Jerry's possession.

Raymond didn't stay very long that second morning, only fifteen minutes. With his head bowed and hands stuffed into his jacket pockets, he hustled across the street to his car, looked up and down Colton Avenue, then got in and drove off.

With a sigh, Fox lifted the iPad from the passenger seat and picked up where he'd left off in *Lawyers Gone Bad*. But as he started reading, his cell phone rang.

The screen on his phone showed the number of Fox's former boss, Dick Reynolds, still the Chief of Global Life and Casualty Insurance's Special Frauds Unit. With a frown, Fox pressed the talk button and said, "Hello? Dick?"

"Hey, Foxy," the Chief said. "Whatcha doing with yourself these days? Want a job?"

Fox had to take a breath and stop himself from laughing.

Chapter Six
The Chief

"What kind of job, Chief?"

Fox had never gotten over calling Dick Reynolds, "Chief." Reynolds had been his boss for almost three years, and he was that kind of hard-nosed, straight-laced law enforcement guy Fox couldn't help but respect. Reynolds had a long, distinguished career with the FBI before coming over to Global to head their newly formed fraud unit more than twenty years ago. The retirement bug hadn't quite caught him yet and, thought Fox, probably never would. He was the type of guy who'd prefer to die of a heart attack at his desk, closing in on an insurance scammer, than spend his last days sleeping late and playing crossword puzzles on a pool deck down in the Villages.

But that wasn't all Fox did in his retirement. He spent some of his extra time writing, working on a novel based on the Jerry Shaw case that he'd tentatively titled, "The Anonymous Man."

He also was putting together the memoirs of his days in the Philly PD. One of his old pals on the force suggested that his thirty years as a detective, mostly spent in the homicide and organized crime bureaus, would make interesting reading. With a laugh, his colleague had told Fox that maybe Hollywood would get hold of his book and make a movie or TV series out of it.

"You heard those two are out, right?" Reynolds asked. "Jeff Flaherty and Holly Shaw. The two that murdered our insured, the husband, Jerry Shaw, and tried to make it look like an accident, to collect the four-mil policy."

"Yeah, I read about it in the papers."

Someone honked the horn for no good reason after passing his space along the curb, and Reynolds asked, "Where are you?"

"On the street," Fox said. "On a job. Staking out a place."

"Cheating husband?"

"Wife," Fox lied. "So what's the job, Chief? Following them? Flaherty and the widow?"

"Yeah, why not? See what they're up to. Maybe they'll lead you to the rest of the money." After a time when Fox didn't say anything, the Chief asked, "Or to Jerry Shaw."

"Jerry Shaw? What, you believe their story, that they really didn't kill him, that he's really not dead and he was in on it with them all along?"

"Sure, why not? I've seen stranger things," the Chief said. "I've been giving it a lot of thought. Maybe, he betrayed them for whatever reason. Set them up in that hotel room down in Florida. Maybe they were having an affair, and he found out about it.

"And, if all that's true," Reynolds went on, "wild as it

seems, if they went after him and found the living, breathing Jerry Shaw, that would lead them to where he stashed the rest of the money. And if we followed them, to us, too."

"About one point three million, we figured, right Chief?" Fox asked.

"Yes," Chief Reynolds agreed. "What's left of the money that Flaherty didn't give us. One point three million dollars. Jerry Shaw's share."

Fox sighed and added, "Well, at least Global got back two-thirds of what they took."

"Well, not quite," corrected Reynolds. "More like a half. As I said, some of it, they spent."

"Half then," Fox said. "Two mil. Better than nothing."

The chief laughed and said, "Good thing Flaherty didn't know he'd be getting out so fast. We'd have gotten nothing."

"But he didn't know that," said Fox. "And at the time, it was a good exchange. Actually, for both him and Holly Shaw."

In exchange for identifying the three out-of-state bank accounts where a little over $2 million of the four they'd taken had been deposited, the DA had recommended a sentence of 25 years to life for Flaherty, rather than life without parole, and 15-25 years for Holly rather than 25-to-life. Thus, Flaherty would be eligible for parole in "only" twenty years and Holly in something like eight. Not all that bad for murdering a man.

"Whether Flaherty and Missus Shaw are lying about faking Jerry Shaw's death," the Chief went on, "and they really did murder him, and tried to make it look like an accident, or whether Jerry Shaw conspired with them to fake his death, there's still a lot of missing money out there. Either way, following them may lead us to it."

Fox thought about that for a time, then said, "Yep. Makes

sense, Chief. Either way, they'll go after the money."

"So, you interested?" Reynolds asked. "They settled in your neck of the woods, though for the life of me I can't understand why you went up to that place to spend the rest of your miserable days, instead of in Philly, or better yet, down in the Villages."

"Buffalo's an up-and-coming city, Chief," Fox said. He ignored Reynolds' laugh on the other end of the call, and added, "And I don't want to spend the rest of my last days becoming a suntanned prune playing shuffleboard and driving a golf cart down in Florida, in what is essentially Heaven's—or Hell's— waiting room."

"Whatever," the chief said. "So, you taking it or what? I'm authorized to double the hourly rate."

Fox pretended to think over the offer for a time. Of course, he wasn't about to take the case. He'd already been hired by Jerry Shaw and thus, taking the case for Global would be a conflict of interest of the worst kind, a complete betrayal of Jerry Shaw and Global, and he wasn't about to do that. Furthermore, the moment he figured out that Jerry had avenged Jeff and Holly's betrayal, he'd become a fan. Jerry no longer seemed like the bad guy. That moniker was reserved for Jerry's nemesis, Jeff Flaherty

Finally, Fox said, "No, sorry Chief. I'm gonna pass. Betty's got too many chores around the house for me to do."

The Chief sighed, his disappointment palpable. "I'm sorry to hear you say no. I was looking forward to working with you again, one last time."

"Got any idea who you gonna assign this case instead of me?" Fox asked. Knowing that would give him a leg up in his representation of Jerry Shaw. He'd know who to look for.

After a pause, the Chief said, "Yeah. Chuck Bruno."

Fox frowned, said nothing. Bruno had been hired about six months after Fox started at Global. Like him, Bruno had come over from the Philly PD after doing his twenty-five years. And like Fox, Bruno had earned a reputation as a relentless investigator who often got his man; however, unlike Fox, Bruno was renowned for cutting corners and doing shady things. It worried Fox that a notoriously unscrupulous hard-charger like Bruno would be, like him, sniffing around to see what Jeff and Holly were up to. At least knowing that Bruno was involved gave him the upper hand, for the time being at least.

"Sure I can't convince you to take it?" the Chief pleaded one last time.

"Yes, I'm sure," replied Fox.

The Chief sighed heavily and said, "Well, if you reconsider, give me a call."

"Sure thing, Chief," Fox said. "But don't hold your breath."

The Chief wished him well and ended the call. A few moments later, Fox perked up when he saw a yellow, Superior Service taxi stop in front of the house where Jeff and Holly were staying and blow the horn.

Chapter Seven
Pete Sharkey

A minute later, Jeff and Holly came walking into view from the back of the house. They strode down the narrow driveway and entered the backseat of the cab. When the cab drove off, Fox followed it.

He stayed a few car lengths behind after the cab turned right from Colton onto Ridge Road. After driving three miles through half the length of Lackawanna, they took the eastbound Thruway. After exiting the Thruway onto Walden Avenue and driving past the sprawling Galleria Mall, Jeff and Holly's cab continued on for another ten minutes until it came to the intersection of Walden and Transit Road and turned left. In three blocks, the cab made a sharp right turn into a small parking lot in front of a two-story, tan-brick office building. As Fox drove past, he saw Jeff and Holly exit the back seat of the cab and walk toward the building. After a quick U-turn a couple blocks further up, Fox drove back toward the building and turned into the lot of a 7-Eleven diagonally across from it. As he pulled in, he noticed that Jeff and Holly's cab was gone.

After turning off the car, Fox grabbed his iPad and searched the online white pages and found that Peter Sharkey & Associates, a private investigations firm, occupied a suite in the building. Fox next found the firm's website. The bio of its owner, Pete Sharkey, indicated that he was a former U. S. Marshal, explaining why the site boasted that, in addition to the usual private investigation services, the firm specialized in finding people: deadbeat dads, stolen children, birth mothers, old high school sweethearts, and other assorted missing persons and fugitives from justice. *We find the living and the presumed dead!* was the firm's motto.

So, that was it, Fox concluded. Jeff and Holly were hiring Pete Sharkey to find Jerry Shaw.

Fox waited an hour and fifteen minutes in the parking lot of the 7-Eleven before another taxi pulled into the parking lot of the building across the street. Moments later, Jeff and Holly exited the building and entered the cab. The cab took them home.

"I think they hired a guy to find you and your money," Fox said to Jerry. He had returned home and settled into his long-time office, a small, square room in the back of the house overlooking a wide lawn and the woods behind it. "Pete Sharkey."

Fox recited Pete Sharkey's impressive credentials. He'd been a federal marshal for over twenty-five years before retiring and starting his own firm. He'd spent most his years in the marshal's service chasing down and capturing all kinds of dangerous fugitives: narcos, murderers, and terrorists.

After Fox finished, Jerry commented, "He sounds like the guy in that movie. The marshal played by Tommy Lee Jones."

"Yep, like that guy," Fox agreed. "Though the most famous federal marshal of all time was Wyatt Earp. They are trained to be real hound dogs. As the motto for Sharkey's firm puts it, 'we find the living and the presumed dead.' You're right up their alley."

After a sigh, Jerry asked, "So now what?"

"Now," Fox replied, "I follow Sharkey around. See where he goes, what he's up to. Oh, another thing, Global's got a man on the case. He's getting tabs on Jeff and Holly as well."

Jerry sighed again and asked, "What do you think this Sharkey fellow will do? Where will he look?"

"Where will he look?" Fox thought a moment. "Where the Anonymous Man got his start, I would guess. In Binghamton."

Chapter Eight
The Search

Pete Sharkey, who had just turned fifty, was a tall, handsome man with a solid athletic build, sandy blond hair, and intense blue eyes. After hearing Jeff and Holly's story as they sat on two leather chairs before the long, uncluttered desk in his wide office, Sharkey leaned forward with a grin and said, "So, it's true, what you told the police. You didn't kill him. You faked his death."

"Yes, he's alive," Jeff said. "Maybe still down in Florida. Maybe near Disney World. And he's got our money. One point three million dollars."

Sharkey leaned back, still grinning, and thought a moment. Finally, he sat forward and said, "And you want me to find him."

"Yeah, that's why we're here," Jeff said. "We want you to find him. And the money."

"But let me get this straight," Sharkey said as he momentarily regarded each of them, first Holly, then Jeff. "The three of you were in on the original deal, faking his death and then collecting the money." He turned to Holly and leered at her. "But then, you betrayed him." He turned to Jeff without a beat, without giving them a chance to answer. "But somehow, he found out, and got his revenge on you first." With a sigh, he sat back again. "That about right?"

Jeff glanced at Holly a moment, then turned to Sharkey and said, "Yea, that's pretty much it. He—he came back from his hiding spot in Binghamton a couple weeks after we faked his death, and somehow found us in bed while he hid in the closet."

Sharkey was frowning now, seeming fascinated, and slightly confused by the story.

"In the closet?"

"Yes, the closet," Holly said. "That's what he told me, later. He hid in the master bedroom closet. He came home that night to see me and snuck upstairs into the bedroom while we were out." She glanced at Jeff and said, "Having dinner I think." She turned back to Sharkey and added, "When we came home, he slipped into the closet, heard us talking."

"Did he hear anything else, besides talking?" Sharkey asked with a knowing smile.

Jeff and Holly both sighed disagreeably.

"What does that matter?" Jeff asked. "The point is he found us out and then set us up for murdering him. Fat prick got his revenge. Only he didn't bank on the prosecutor screwing up. He didn't count on us getting out of prison. Whatever happened before that doesn't matter. The only thing that matters is us finding him and getting the rest of the goddamned money. Our goddamned money."

"Well, you mean Global's money."

Jeff shrugged as if he didn't see it that way.

"Or should I say, what's left of Global's money," Sharkey said. "Because, as I recall it, you gave away your share to get a sentence reduction. Two million dollars for twenty-five to life."

"Right," Jeff said with a nod. "I had no other choice."

"Only, as it turns out, ironically, you didn't need to do it," Sharkey went on. "Did you?"

Jeff looked down and grumbled, "No."

Sharkey emitted a little laugh for a moment, then turned serious. He leaned forward again, and said, "Okay, I'll do it. Find Jerry Shaw for you."

Jeff looked up and said, "And your fee for that is?"

"Of the one point three million?" Sharkey leaned back and stared up for a time with the fingers of his right hand tapping on his lower lip. Finally, he looked at Jeff and said, "A third of whatever I collect."

Jeff did a quick calculation. Could be a little over four hundred grand, depending on how much Jerry had burned through in two years.

"First, I gotta find him," Sharkey said. "A person who's dead to the world, invisible."

"Anonymous," Holly whispered.

"What was that?" Sharkey asked her.

She cleared her throat and stated, "Anonymous. That's what he's become. Like the comic book superhero he invented, The Anonymous Man."

Sharkey frowned at Holly as if she was talking nonsense. "Yeah, sure, anonymous, invisible, whatever. The point is, he's disappeared, maybe to Florida, as you say. And everyone considers him dead." He sighed. "We have to hope he stayed where he was, near Disney World, even after you found him. Maybe he felt safe with you in prison and stayed down there." He looked at them with a frown. "And he's down there with, what did you say? A whore?"

"Yes, whore, escort," Holly said, and she spat the name, "Jade."

"She have a last name?"

Holly shook her head and said, "Not that we know of," and Sharkey smirked and went back to thinking about the case.

"Even if I find him," Sharkey finally went on, "and his whore, this Jade, I still gotta make him tell me where the money is—where he's stashed it, what bank accounts, securities, what not." He frowned and added, "Yeah, to do all that is easily worth a third."

After thinking about it a moment, Jeff sighed and said, "Alright. A third of whatever we get out of Jerry." After another sigh, he asked, "Where you gonna start? Where they caught us? Kissimmee?"

"No," Sharkey said. "Binghamton. I always start at the beginning, where the trail starts."

Holly shook his head and said, "It's gonna be tough. Like I said, he's anonymous."

Sharkey glared at her and said, "No one who's alive is truly anonymous. No one."

Chapter Nine
Snakes

"But first, I need more information," Sharkey said. "And you can start by telling me more about this whore, Jade.

"All we know is Jerry met her in Binghamton," Holly said. "At some point, they left and moved to Florida. To Kissimmee, to be exact. Like we said, near Disney."

"Looks just like Holly," Jeff chimed in.

Holly turned to him with a scowl and said, "No, she doesn't."

"Oh, yes, she does." Jeff looked at Sharkey. "They are like twin sisters, Holly and her. Jade's his front."

"His front?"

"Yeah, his front," Jeff explained. "The person through whom he—a dead man, anonymous, or whatever—interacts with the world." He nodded at Holly. "In our plan, Holly was to be that for Jerry, down in Binghamton, his front."

"But first she betrayed him," Sharkey said and smiled.

Holly looked down sheepishly. After a moment, she looked up and said, "Jeff and I, we fell in love."

Sharkey frowned at that pronouncement as Jeff glanced at Holly and smiled. *Odd, these two,* he thought. He recalled reading in the papers, back when the case was big local news, that Holly had testified against Jeff to get her deal. He turned and looked at Jeff as Jeff stared into Holly's eyes. Sharkey wondered if Jeff had truly forgiven Holly's betrayal. Or perhaps, Holly was working some scam on Jeff. Even if she wasn't, right at this moment, Sharkey wouldn't put it past her to double-cross Jeff again. And vice-versa. It seemed part of their genetic make-up. Survival is what motivated them. Just like snakes. Two snakes that could not be trusted.

"So he met this Jade in Binghamton," Sharkey went on. "You know how?"

"She advertised in one of those artsy magazines down there," Jeff said and turned to Holly. "Right?"

"That's what Jerry told me," Holly said. "He got lonely, horny, whatever, when he first went down there after we faked his death. He found her ad, called her. She came over, stayed the night."

"That had to cost him," Sharkey commented with a laugh.

Ignoring that, Holly continued, "Then, somewhere along the way, I'm not sure how or why he developed feelings for her."

"Jerry boy fell in love," Jeff chimed in. He turned to Holly and said, "Because she looks so much like you. Your twin."

"Whatever," she said with a shrug and looked back at Sharkey. "All I know is that he fell in love or something, and then he set us up with the incriminating emails, made it look like we killed him for the insurance money.

"But then you and Jerry made up," Jeff reminded her as he sat forward. "Or pretended to."

"Yeah, pretended," Holly said, then turned to Sharkey. "We met up during the first trial in Buffalo. He approached me. Then, once he figured out that the Global insurance investigator was following him, and us…"

"Fox," Jeff interrupted. "Jack Fox."

"Yeah, Fox. Once he learned that Fox was following him, wondering what his connection to me and Jerry Shaw was, he decided we should run for it."

"By then," Jeff added, "he looked nothing like the old Jerry. He'd lost weight."

"Yeah, finally," Holly said and laughed to herself. "He lost weight. Lots of weight. He'd worked himself into shape. After all those years trying." She sighed thinking about how good Jerry had looked when he'd surprised her in the parking garage across the street from the courthouse that afternoon. "Anyway, he drove me down to Kissimmee and put me up in a cheap hotel." She looked over at Jeff and smiled. "That's when I called Jeff. And then he came down…"

"To kill him," Sharkey guessed. "To kill Jerry."

"Well, yeah," Jeff said. "We had no other choice."

"But that obviously didn't happen," Sharkey said.

"No," Jeff answered. "His fucking whore, Jade, rescued him. And that led to our arrest down there. And the rest, as they say, is history. Year and a half later, we're sitting here, hiring you to find Jerry."

"And the money."

"Yeah, and the money," Jeff agreed. "Most of all, that."

Sharkey sighed and thought a minute, convinced more than

ever that Jeff and Holly were snakes. Finally, he leaned forward and said, "You said Jerry went down there, to Binghamton, right after you faked his death."

"Yeah, right after," Jeff said. "Late October, two years ago."

"And he met Jade shortly after that?"

"Yes," Jeff said. After glancing at Holly, he added, "The first night he was down here, I think," and Holly nodded.

"And you don't know her last name?"

"No," Holly said, "we don't. Jerry just told me, Jade."

Sharkey sighed and leaned back in his chair. He thought for a time, then leaned forward and said, "Well, that gives me something, a start. Though not much of one. Jerry Shaw's connected to an escort who went by the name, Jade, who worked in Binghamton around two years ago and advertised her services in an artsy paper before she ended up becoming his front, the Anonymous Man's front. Is that about it?"

Jeff nodded and said, "Yeah, that's about it. So, you think you can find him just based on that?"

Sharkey smiled and said, "Like our motto says, if he's alive, we'll find him."

Chapter Ten
Binghamton

At six-thirty the following morning, Pete Sharkey woke up in his half-million-dollar house in an upscale neighborhood along a private golf course in Clarence, just north of Buffalo. He took a quick shower, dressed in jeans and a polo shirt, then quietly went to the spacious, open kitchen and brewed a pot of coffee, careful not to waken his wife of twenty-five years who remained gently snoring on her side of the king-sized bed in their spacious master bedroom. The night before, he'd told her that he'd be out of town for a few days. Not where, of course. He never told her that, though he did promise to call that evening and check up on her and their two pre-teen daughters.

Sharkey filled his favorite cup from the pot of strong Colombian he had just brewed and stood munching a buttered hard roll while leaning on the quartz top of the center aisle. After pouring the remaining coffee into a stainless-steel mug, he left the house to start his three-and-a-half hour drive to Binghamton in his Lexus RX SUV.

By eleven that morning, Sharkey was checking into a Holiday Inn off Vestal Parkway across the street from the main entrance to Binghamton University. When Jerry and Holly Shaw had attended college there, now over ten years ago, it had been called SUNY Binghamton. Years earlier, in the nineteen-sixties, it had been a small, staid private school known as Harpur College.

It was noon by the time Sharkey settled in, washed up, and brushed his teeth. Lunch could wait. Instead, he drove three miles east from the hotel on Vestal Parkway and turned into a strip mall where *The Tri-Cities Arts & Leisure* occupied one of the storefronts. The weekly paper covered the theatre, music and art scene of the so-called Tri-Cities of Binghamton, Johnson City, and Endicott, bordering the meandering Susquehanna River in south-central New York State. Like most northern rust-belt metropolises, it had seen better days. In addition to articles of local interest to the art scene, the liberal editors of the paper inserted political attack pieces against conservative local, state and national politicians and their causes.

A fortyish, tall, thin black man greeted Sharkey with a smirk from behind a chest-high counter of the cramped lobby. Beyond the counter, Sharkey saw several unoccupied desks cluttered with various documents, old editions of the paper, and other newspapers.

"Can I help you?" the employee asked with a slight lisp and Sharkey immediately thought, *gay*.

Without giving a reason, Sharkey asked if he could look through back issues of the paper from October two years previous. The employee thought a moment, then with a small shrug, said, "Sure. It may take a few minutes, if I can find them."

Twenty minutes later, after sifting through stacks of papers in a back room, his search interrupted by several phone calls, the employee brought out two weekly editions of the paper and placed them on the counter before Sharkey.

"These are them," he said. "October. What are you looking for? Maybe I can help you find it."

With a scowl, thinking, *gay*, again, Sharkey shook his head and said, "No, I'll find it." After a shrug, the employee stepped away from the counter and returned to a desk against the far wall and continued whatever he'd been doing when Sharkey walked in.

Sharkey flipped to the back pages of the first paper and immediately found what he was looking for—an escort ad for Jerry Shaw's Jade among the classifieds.

Exotic, exciting, pleasurable, call Jade.

Locally, outcalls only 24/7, 200, no tips, 333-8112.

A small, blurry photograph was to the right of the ad, depicting Jade. With a nod, Sharkey agreed with Jeff Flaherty that Jade could indeed pass for Holly Shaw's twin.

After checking the other edition of the paper that had come out after Holly and Jeff and Jerry had faked Jerry's death, Sharkey found the same ad. He raised a hand to get the employee's attention but had to wait as the phone rang yet again. After ending the call, the employee asked, "Did you find what you were looking for?"

"Yes, I did," Sharkey said. "It's an ad. Can I ask you a couple questions about it?"

The employee got up from behind his desk and sauntered

over to the counter. Sharkey pointed out the ad and the employee frowned and said, "Oh, it's one of those. We stopped taking them about a year ago." He looked up and gave Sharkey a tight smile. "They're sex ads."

Sharkey ignored that and asked, "Is there a record of who placed it? Who paid for it?"

"From two years ago? I doubt it. Our accountant might have it. He works downtown. In Binghamton. You might check with him."

Sharkey thought a moment. As a last resort, he might just do that.

"Could I get a copy of the ad?"

The employee shrugged and said, "Sure." He took the paper to an old, bulky copy machine against the side wall, placed the page face down on it, and pressed a button. A moment later, he brought the sheet with the copied page to Sharkey.

Sharkey examined it a moment and said, "Thanks."

"Can I help you with anything else?"

"No, that's it."

As Sharkey turned to leave, the employee asked, "You know her or something, the girl?"

Sharkey stopped and looked back at the employee. "Huh?"

"The girl in the ad. You know her?"

At first, Sharkey thought of telling the employee it was none of his business. Instead, he said, "Yeah, she's a friend. I'm looking for her."

"Well, hope you find her." The guy sighed. "That's no kind of life."

Neither is being gay, Sharkey thought, but instead, he replied, "Yeah, me too." *And it's worth a million bucks to me if I do,* he added to himself as he turned and walked out of the place.

Chapter Eleven
Julio Gonzalez

Back in his hotel room, after downing a quarter-pounder and fries from a nearby McDonald's, Sharkey powered up his laptop and quickly found the owner of the cell phone number in Jade's two-year-old escort ad had been one Julio Gonzalez. He used a search website to find Julio's current address, 271 Larkin Street in Johnson City, together with his current cell phone number and email address.

From a couple other sites, Sharkey learned that Julio was thirty-eight years old, was five-foot-seven, weighed one-hundred seventy-five pounds, had dark brown hair, brown eyes and various tattoos on his arms and neck. He had a record, though nothing much: State convictions for selling marijuana, assault, criminal trespass reduced from a burglary charge, and three raps for promoting prostitution. He'd never done time, though he was currently on probation. One site provided

Sharkey with several mugshots depicting a swarthy Latino with narrow eyes and a pock-marked face. Now, Sharkey knew what Jade's former pimp looked like.

The search took nearly an hour and invigorated Sharkey. From his years at the U.S. Marshal's service, he had honed the art of finding people who didn't want to get found. His mentor had been Ed Bailey, a crusty old agent with almost forty years of service behind him. Ed had once told him that a good marshal becomes a predator of humans; and, like all predators, the hunt was the thrill. But these days, Bailey had grumbled, the internet had made the hunt far too easy. In the old days, you had to search court and county records and often scour the streets. Now, you didn't even have to lift your ass off your goddamned chair to find someone. Still, for Sharkey, whether doing it the old-fashioned way or using modern techniques, the chase remained a thrill. When the prey was sighted, and you crept within sufficient reach to snatch him or her, the heart pounded and the mind focused. One tasted blood. It must have been the same way a lion felt stalking an antelope or a gazelle.

Finding Julio Gonzalez was one thing, but finding the so-called Anonymous Man promised to be quite another. Jerry Shaw was a special kind of prey whose life had been designed to avoid detection; and, in this case, he knew that Jeff and Holly were coming after him. That knowledge would make Jerry even more cautious and thus make the task of finding him all the more difficult. Sharkey hoped that Jerry hadn't been proactive and already knew that Jeff and Holly had hired him to find his trail. Still, a good hunter had to consider that possibility and plan the hunt accordingly.

The first step on the trail of finding Jerry Shaw had been taken. Sharkey had found Jade's pimp. Although he assumed that Julio wouldn't likely know exactly where Jade had run off to, he might be able to provide crucial information that could help Sharkey find her, and through her, him—the man she fronted for, the Anonymous Man. For instance, Julio might know Jade's last name, the identity and location of relatives—a mother and father, perhaps—as well as siblings, cousins, friends and who knew what else.

Larkin Street was in an older section of Johnson City that, like most of that city's neighborhoods over the last fifty years, had seen better days. IBM, Endicott Shoes and many other manufacturers and businesses had long ago closed shop and left town, taking good jobs with them. When the jobs left, the honest, taxpaying workers also left town. What remained were those too poor or too dumb to leave, broken families, and the criminal element that prayed on them. The streets were soon overrun by drug dealers, gangs and pimps, and the nice little houses once occupied by law-abiding workers soon fell into disrepair.

Around five that evening, wearing jeans, a polo shirt, and a jacket, Sharkey walked onto the slightly off-kilter wooden porch of the hulking, clapboard house at 271 Larkin Street. Without hesitation, he pounded on the front door of the lower unit. Waiting for someone to answer, he glanced at an old, rusty, beat-up Toyota Corolla parked halfway down the narrow, cracked, weed-infested asphalt driveway along the right side of the house. Grass and weeds were also growing along the bottom of its peeling concrete foundation.

Sharkey pounded three more times before the thick, wooden front door finally opened enough for a Hispanic girl in her late teens wearing jeans and halter-top to peek out at him.

She frowned, then asked, "Help you, mister?"

"Julio there?"

Her frown deepened as she glared out at him.

"Look, I know he's there," Sharkey said. "And he'll want to talk to me. Tell him it's about Jade."

She gave a small shrug, glanced back into the house. Finally, an arm pushed her aside, and the door squeaked open. Suddenly, a squat, dark man with a pockmarked face wearing jeans and no top appeared before Sharkey in an aggressive stance. His hair was disheveled, and his look was mean. Tattoos looking like smudge marks of something nasty covered his arms and neck.

"You want something, Mister?"

"You know a girl named Jade?"

Frowning, Julio said, "Jade? No."

"I think you do," Sharkey said. "I think you and her used to do business together."

"Yeah, maybe; so, you a cop or something?"

Sharkey smirked, reached into his jacket pocket and handed Julio his business card. Frowning, Julio looked at it. The card said, "Pete Sharkey, Private Investigator." Finally, Julio looked up. With a shrug, he said, "Yeah, so?"

"I'm trying to find her," Sharkey said. "Jade."

"Like I said, I don't know no Jade."

"Look, cut the bullshit," Sharkey said. "I ain't no cop, and I could care less that Jade once turned tricks for you. All I want is for you to help me find her."

Julio glared at Sharkey for a time, and seemed to relax. He sighed and said, "I don't know where the fuck she is. She took off. Haven't seen her in like two years. Bitch owes me money."

"How much?"

With a shrug, Julio said, "Few hundred."

"Well, maybe if you help me," Sharkey said, "I can get you what she owes."

Julio nodded, smiled as if unimpressed by the claim and said, "Whatever. So, what do you want to know? Like I said, I haven't seen her in two years."

"You can start by telling me her last name," Sharkey said.

Julio frowned, thinking. He looked up and said, "Martin. Jade Martin."

"She got family in town?"

"No, no family. She told me once her father was dead and that she'd run away from a step-father hitting on her or something, that kind of shit."

"Know where she ran from?"

"No, man," Julio said and laughed. "New York, maybe. I mean, they don't fill out a job application or nothing."

"She have any girlfriends when she was here, working for you?"

"Yeah, she had a girlfriend. Her best friend, Faith Smith. And that bitch owes me money, too."

"This Faith Smith, she still in town?"

"No, man. That bitch took off, too. Like three, four months ago. I heard that she went to live with Jade. Down in Florida."

"How do you know that?"

"Her grandma told me."

Chapter Twelve
Postmark

Julio told Sharkey that Faith's grandmother's name was Sylvia Dinardo. He described her as a gnarly, skanky woman who lived only a few blocks away on Keller Street with a granddaughter and her baby.

"She told me a hundred times Faith ran off to Florida to be with Jade," Julio went on. "She don't know where. And fuck, I believe her." After a laugh, he added, "She just don't know. I'm sure of that." How he was sure of that, he didn't say. But Sharkey imagined that he'd played rough early on with Faith's grandmother, maybe putting a pistol to her head or to the head of someone she loved. "Still, that bitch Faith owes me two fucking grand. Got her fucking teeth fixed. Then, out of nowhere, she takes off. You find her, and that other one, Jade, get the money, I'll give you a cut."

"Sure thing, Mister Gonzalez," Sharkey said with a frown.

"Sure thing."

Ten minutes later, Sharkey was standing on Sylvia Dinardo's porch, cluttered with broken chairs and soiled plastic toys, another old, hulking clapboard house in a decaying Johnson City neighborhood. He had knocked several times before the door creaked open and the fearful eyes of a toddler wearing only a droopy diaper peered up at him.

"Your grandma home?"

The sad little boy just stood there peering up at Sharkey. From inside, Sharkey heard a woman yell, "Jorgie, get away from there." A moment later, a fat girl with oily, frizzled red hair, pimply dark skin, wearing a slinky sweat-suit that parts of her were falling out of, appeared at the crack in the door.

"Help you, Mister?"

"Sylvia Dinardo here?" Sharkey asked. "It's about her granddaughter, Faith."

The girl turned around and yelled to Sylvia, "Grandma, some man's here about Faith." She turned to Sharkey and said, "Faith don't live here no more."

"I know," Sharkey said with a tight smile.

A minute later, a smoke-skinny, beat-up looking woman in her late fifties wearing a wrinkled house dress was at the door. "Faith don't live here no more," the woman said with a scowl and a gravelly voice from smoking too much. She squinted at Sharkey and asked. "She okay?"

"As far as I know, yeah," Sharkey said. "She's okay. I'm trying to find her, make sure of that."

"Well, I don't know where she is. She ran off to. Went down to Florida somewhere is all I know." She squinted at Sharkey again. "You a cop?"

"No, I'm not a cop," Sharkey said. "I'm a private investigator. I work for someone looking for Faith's friend, Jade Martin. I heard Faith went down to Florida to live with Jade."

The woman frowned disagreeably and asked, "That spic Julio send you?"

"Look, I don't work for Julio. I work for someone else. They hired me to find Jade, not Faith, but maybe Faith can lead me to her."

After frowning at Sharkey for a time, the woman said, "Yeah, she left and went down there, to Florida, to be with Jade. To get away from Julio. But I don't know where she's at down there."

"She ever contact you? Call?"

After thinking things over, the woman asked, "So she's not in trouble, is she? Faith?"

"No, I told you, this isn't about Faith, it's about Jade."

After a sigh, the woman decided something and said, "Yeah, she called a couple times. When she first took off, few months back."

"And that's it?" Sharkey asked. "Your only contact, a couple phone calls?"

She thought a moment, then added, "Well, a couple weeks back, she sent me a letter. Said she's alright. Sent me some money."

"You still have it? This letter?"

The woman nodded and left Sharkey standing at the door. When she returned moments later, she handed Sharkey an envelope and said, "Here. Don't say much."

Sharkey saw the woman's name and address neatly handprinted across the front of the envelope in blue ink. There was no return address. From inside it, he pulled out a single page of unlined copy paper on which Faith, presumably, had written a brief note in a neat, straight script, also in blue ink. There was a date from three weeks ago printed on the top right side of the page. The woman was right—the note didn't say much. But Sharkey read it anyway, twice.

Hi Grandma,

Just wanted to tell you I'm okay. I'm still living with Jade down here. I still can't tell you where. Just know, I'm fine. I'm working at a Denny's the last month, making some money. And I'm even taking online college courses. I think maybe I want to become a physician's assistant. Anyway, I'm sending you a hundred dollars.

I know Debbie and Jorgie are staying with you. I miss you a lot. Someday maybe I can come home and visit. But not right now. Not until that Julio stops looking for me. Maybe, pretty soon, I can pay him back the money I owe him. Shut up his ugly face calling me names. Okay, gotta go. Hope you are well, and your arthritis is okay. I'll write again soon, send you more money when I can.

Love,
Faith

"See," the woman said when Sharkey looked up. "Don't say much."

No, Sharkey thought, *it says a lot*. For one thing, it confirmed that Faith was still living with Jade and Jerry Shaw. And now he knew that Faith worked at a Denny's somewhere in Florida. But there must be hundreds of Denny's in Florida. Sharkey looked at the front of the envelope, read the smudged postmark, and smiled.

"You mind if I take this, the envelope?" Sharkey asked the woman.

With a shrug, she said, "Yeah, sure."

"You got a picture of her somewhere? Of Faith?"

Again, the woman left him standing on the porch and went back into the dark house. A minute or so later, she returned and handed Sharkey a creased photograph depicting an attractive enough girl standing in the front yard of someone's house. Her pose was confident, determined. She wore a strapless dress and too much makeup on her pretty, long, thin face.

"That's from a couple years back," the woman said. "I don't have too many pictures."

Sharkey commented, "Pretty girl." *Nice bod*, he thought. He looked up at the woman and said, "Takes after her grandma." The woman shrugged.

"You really think you can find her, Mister?"

"I'll try."

"You do," she said. "You tell her to come home."

Back in his car, along the curb in front of Sylvia Dinardo's house, Sharkey examined the postmark on the envelope. After confirming that it bore a date three weeks ago, he also noted, more importantly, that the letter had been received for delivery at the Loughman Post Office. Using his smartphone, he found that this particular post office was located on Ronald Reagan Parkway in Davenport, Florida, in northeast Polk County, about fifteen minutes from Disney World.

Sharkey next searched the Denny's website for the locations within a twenty-five-mile radius of Davenport. He found only four. He smiled. The scent of his prey was growing stronger. When he found Faith, she'd lead him to Jade Martin and, of course, after that, to the Anonymous Man.

Chapter Thirteen
Update

"He's in Binghamton," Fox said.

Fox was sitting in his car parked in the lot in front of the Holiday Inn on Vestal Parkway where Sharkey was staying. Fox told Jerry what he'd seen Sharkey do that day—his early morning drive down to Binghamton; his immediate visit to the offices of the *Tri-Cities Arts & Leisure* weekly paper; and, finally, that evening, his meetings and interviews with Julio Gonzalez and Sylvia Dinardo.

"Julio was Jade's manager," Jerry said.

"Pimp, you mean."

"Yeah, pimp. But that's over now."

"Do you know who the woman was?" Fox asked.

"Faith's grandmother."

"Who's Faith?"

"She's Jade's best friend," Jerry said. "From her days up

there. They both worked for Julio. After Jade came down here with me, she kept in touch with Faith. Then, about four months ago, Faith wanted to get away from Julio, from that life, so Jade told her to come down here, hide out for a while, change her life."

"Hide behind the cloak of the Anonymous Man," Fox suggested.

"Yeah, something like that," Jerry said. "Anyway, that's what Faith did, came down here. And she's been down here ever since. Now, she's about ready to come out from behind my cloak, go off on her own. Any day, now." Jerry sighed and asked, "So what's he want with her grandmother?"

"It's obvious," Fox said. "If he finds Faith, he finds you. The grandmother may be able to tell him where Faith is."

"He figured out that Faith is here, with us? How?"

"I told you," Fox said. "He's a former U.S. Marshal. That's what they do. Find people."

"But Julio and Faith's grandmother don't know where she is down here," Jerry suggested. "Florida's a big state."

"The old woman showed Sharkey a letter," Fox said. "At least I think that's what it was through my binoculars, though my eyes aren't so good anymore. You have to ask Faith if she sent her grandmother a letter."

"I'll do that," Jerry said. "But she's at work. When I pick her up. What time is it?"

"Eight-thirty."

"She works 'til ten," Jerry said. "I'm picking her up then."

"Where's she work?"

"At a Denny's ten minutes from here."

"She wouldn't be, well, unsophisticated enough to have given her grandmother a return address in that letter she sent her?"

"No, of course not," Jerry said. "She's not stupid. She knows how important staying anonymous is for me, and Jade, and her. So, you think there's anything to worry about now that he's connected Faith to us? Down here?"

"I don't know," Fox admitted. "Depends on whether he gleaned anything from Faith's letter to her grandmother. Let's hope she didn't say anything that could give your location away. I saw Sharkey leave with an envelope, probably the envelope the letter came in. Even if there wasn't a return address, there'd be a postmark."

"So what?"

"A postmark will tell him what post office the letter was mailed from," Fox said.

"Really?"

"Yes, really," Fox said. "And where would that be? Your local post office."

"Loughman, I think, something like that," Jerry said. "We don't mail any letters. But I know one's there."

"How far is that from you?"

"A few miles."

Fox thought for a time, then said, "Still, it doesn't give him much. Finding a post office and your house is still like looking for a needle in a haystack, although the haystack just got a little smaller than the entire state of Florida."

"So we don't have to worry?"

"No, I didn't say that," Fox said. "You have to worry. Exercise due care. For now, he's still here, in Binghamton, twelve hundred miles from you. He'll probably spend a little while longer sniffing around. Trying to find your scent."

"How do you know that?"

"That's what hunters do."

Chapter Fourteen
Ambushed

"Can I ask you something, Mister Fox?" Jerry said.

"Call me Jack."

"Okay, Jack. Why you doing this? I mean, I always wondered why. What did you get out of letting me go?"

"Why?" Fox thought for a time. Finally, he laughed and said, "You know, I wonder that, too. Maybe I admired you a little bit, how you got your revenge on Jeff and Holly. Maybe I see them as the bad guys; and, I thought it only just that they did time for the killing they really did commit."

"The body guy," Jerry said. "Willie Robinson."

"Yeah, him. It was them, right?"

"Yes." Jerry sighed. "Jeff killed him. I was too late to stop him. Jeff stabbed him in the back. Holly was just as guilty. She knew he was going to do it and let him. Robinson was blackmailing us, wanted more money for what he did. Plus, he was a witness. I was next."

"So you took out your revenge," Fox said. "Got even with them by setting them up for your murder." He laughed. "That was a neat deal. That's what I admired. Only, you almost ruined it by getting back with her, Holly."

Jerry remained quiet for a time.

"You still love her," Fox added, "don't you?"

Jerry sighed and considered the question for a time. Finally, he said, "I don't know how I feel about her."

"Even after everything she's done to you," Fox said. "Her multiple betrayals."

"We have a lot of history," Jerry replied dryly. "Ten years, seven of them married."

"And where does Jade fit into all that history?"

"I love her," Jerry said. "I know that."

"Do you?"

"Yes." Jerry brought up an image of Jade in his mind. She was off feeding the baby now, in the nursery, rocking him in her arms as he slowly finished his bottle. He thought of how closely Jade resembled Holly and wondered again if that was the only reason why he cared for her. No! he told himself. He loved Jade for being Jade.

"Well, just remember who's been true to you and who hasn't," Fox advised.

Jerry didn't have to be told. Jade had saved his life, and Holly had tried to take it from him.

"Ultimately," Fox went on, "I think I was right about you. You're a good egg."

"Yeah, how did you come to that conclusion?"

"I think, no, I know, you sent Willie Robinson's wife some money for one thing. It fell out of the sky. An envelope came, no return address, with a certified check in it drawn on some bank account in Illinois, in the name of a New Mexican LLC."

"How do you know that?"

"I went to see her," Fox said. "After what happened down in Florida, I had a hunch as to what was really going on. Plus, from that time I glanced at you in the courtroom, something was itching at the back of my brain. The truth."

"Well, you were right. Is that why you were at my fake gravestone in the cemetery on my birthday?" Jerry asked. "Another hunch?"

"Yeah, my hunches are often right."

"What's your hunch tell you this time? About Sharkey and them finding me?"

"That's what's bothering me," Fox said. "I don't have one."

Fox promised to call Jerry the next night to give him an update on what Sharkey was up to, and especially whether he was on his way down to Florida, to the area around the Loughman Post Office.

"You'll be the first to know if that happens," Fox promised him. "Look, until then, I'll send you a couple pictures I snapped of Sharkey. You ever see him, you run and hide."

Fox had used his long-range digital video camera to take several snapshots of Sharkey on the prowl, leaving and returning to the lobby of the Holiday Inn, entering the Arts and Leisure offices, and chatting with Julio Gonzalez and Sylvia Dinardo. He had sent them to his photographs app on his smartphone and now sent them to Jerry Shaw's prepaid cell phone. Now, at least, Jerry would have an idea what the guy stalking him looked like.

"Got them, Mister Fox."

"Jack."

"Jack. And one more thing."

"What's that?"

"Thanks."

After the call, Fox sat in the parking lot for another half hour, watching the entrance to the lobby of the hotel. Finally, he figured Sharkey was done for the night and after a yawn, he exited the car. He'd taken a room in the hotel as well. Sharkey had no idea who he was, and he felt it more convenient being close to the target of his surveillance than staying at another place.

After a moment leaning up against the car in the now deserted, dark parking lot on a chilly, quiet night, Fox started for the lobby. After three or four steps, he heard something in the shadows behind him, a footstep perhaps. He stopped, turned slightly, listened for a moment and out of the corner of his left eye, he noticed a figure.

Something hard slapped across the left side of his face, and Fox heard the horrific, dull thud of his own skull being cracked. The pain was momentary as he fell sideways onto the asphalt. He felt a hand reach into the back pocket of his jeans to pluck out his wallet.

And, then, nothing.

Chapter Fifteen
Something's Wrong

Jerry didn't hear from Fox the next night, and that worried him. The following morning, he confided his concern to Jade. "Something's wrong," he said to her at the kitchen table as they ate a pile of pancakes Jade had made. The baby had just slurped down a bottle and was back napping in his crib.

Jade knew the situation. Jerry had hired Fox and that Fox had followed Holly and Jeff to an appointment with Pete Sharkey, a former U. S. Marshal and thus an expert at finding missing persons and fugitives; and, that Sharkey was now working for Holly and Jeff to find Jerry and her. She also knew that Fox had followed Sharkey to Binghamton and watched him interview Julio Gonzalez and Faith's grandmother; and, that Fox had called Jerry a couple nights back to update him on his observations.

"He should've called by now," Jerry said.

"Did you call him?"

Jerry poured more syrup on what remained of his pancakes and shook his head.

"Not yet," Jerry said.

"Why not?"

"I don't know. Being extra-cautious." He thought a moment and sighed. To stay anonymous, an anonymous man had to be careful, exercise extreme vigilance. "Maybe something happened. Maybe his phone fell into the wrong hands."

"What wrong hands?"

Jerry suddenly pushed his plate away. He looked up at Jade with worry in his eyes.

"Into the hands of that guy," he said. "Sharkey. And if he's got it and picked up if I called, he'd realize it was me. He'd have my number."

"And how would he have come by Fox's phone?"

"I have no idea."

"But if he's got Fox's phone," Jade said, "he'd have your number anyway. And so what? Your number leads nowhere, to no one."

Jade was right. That was the beauty of a prepaid cell phone. It was untraceable.

"Try him."

Jerry shrugged and after a moment, fished his phone out of his pocket and clicked Fox's number on the contact list. Within moments, Fox's cell was ringing. After four rings, somebody answered, "Hello." It wasn't Fox's voice. "Hello? Who's this?"

Jerry promptly clicked the end-call button. He looked across at Jade and said, "Somebody's got his phone."

"So you were right," Jade said. "Something's wrong."

"Jesus." Jerry took in a breath and tried to think. Finally, he looked at Jade again and said, "We need to leave."

"You think?"

"Yes," he said. "Get a room at a nice hotel, that Marriot near the main gate. Hide out for a few days until this blows over."

"What about the baby, Faith?"

"You can take the baby," he said. "Bring the pac-n-play. And I'll get Faith a separate room."

"You sure we need to do that?" Jade asked. "Upset our lives like that? That guy they hired to talk to Julio and Faith's grandmother. So what? They don't have the slightest idea where we are."

"We should have moved out of Florida after they got arrested. Gone to California."

"Why? We couldn't have foreseen them getting out."

"Still, I think we should hide out for a while," Jerry argued. "Fox said that guy Holly and Jeff hired is real good, an expert at finding people, even an anonymous man. And Fox being disengaged from his phone cinches it for me. What do we have to lose by laying low for a few days, hiding out?"

"Leading normal lives, that's what," Jade argued. "And how long we gonna be doing this? Running, hiding? A week, a month, forever? When's it... what did you say? When's it gonna blow over?"

Jerry sighed and said, "I don't know." He sighed again and decided that was wrong, he did know. "Maybe when Holly and Jeff are gone. Out of our lives, permanently."

"And how do you make that happen? You gotta a plan for that?"

"No, not right at this moment," Jerry admitted. "The best

plan I have for the time being is for you and the baby and Faith to get out of here, and for me to go find out what happened to Fox."

"What, up in Buffalo?"

"Yeah, up in Buffalo. I don't see what other choice we have. Do you?"

After a time, Jade shook her head and said, "No, you need to go on up there. Shuffle off to Buffalo."

Chapter Sixteen
Shuffling Off

"But before I leave," Jerry said, "I have to get you and the baby, and Faith, into a safe space."

Jade reluctantly agreed, and they selected a Fairfield Inn on Vineland Road not far from the Premium Outlets about fifteen minutes from Disney World. There was a good deal for the relatively slow time of late October, only $80 a night. Jerry called and booked two rooms for three nights. Jerry begged and got them a room at Noon rather than the usual three p.m. registration.

It was only ten, so they had two hours to kill.

"Let's get the baby and walk around the outlets," Jerry said. "Then, get you into the room."

"What about Faith? She's working until ten tonight."

"Text her and tell her what we're doing. I'll still pick her up, and take her to the Fairfield. After a good night's sleep—

hopefully, Seius will allow that—I'll start the drive north an hour or so before daybreak, six or so."

"Straight through?"

"Yes," Jerry said. "If I can. We need to get to the bottom of this soon as we can." That meant a twenty-hour trip up north along a series of interstates. The final leg was the New York State Thruway, I-90, about an hour to Buffalo from the Pennsylvania line.

Jerry booked a room for the following night at the Stadium Inn in Orchard Park on US 20, out by New Era Stadium where the Buffalo Bills played. Fortunately, the Bills were out of town that Sunday and the motel was cheap, $55 a night. It was also convenient to everything, close to Jack Fox's house and not far from the upper flat in Lackawanna, Jerry's former hometown, where Holly and Jeff were currently staying. It was also the same motel where he'd spent a couple nights after he and Holly and Jeff had faked his death, enabling him to watch his fictitious wake and funeral.

"Just promise you'll stop if you get tired," Jade said to him as she patted his hand across the kitchen table. "I don't need Jerry Shaw really dead."

At ten to ten that night, Jerry pulled into the parking lot of the Denny's on US 27 next to a Pilot Travel Center, essentially a gas station and convenience store catering primarily to long-distance truckers, about six miles from the I-4 interchange. Faith had worked there for the last month or so. The restaurant was only ten minutes from Jerry and Jade's house, and she found the work easy enough with decent tips from truckers and tourists and snowbirds. The job also gave her time to enroll in online courses at Polk State College in a program toward becoming a physician's assistant.

Jerry parked in a spot at the far end of the lot well beyond the gas pumps where cars swung in at all hours of the day and night to fill up. It was also beyond where truckers constantly pulled in their rigs and took one of the many long spaces behind the main building that housed the convenience store and attached Denny's. Before Holly and Jeff had been released from prison, he'd have driven up and parked in a spot nearest the front entrance of the restaurant and wait outside the car. When Faith came out, he'd wave her over. But with Holly and Jeff, through Pete Sharkey, on the prowl after him, Jerry was more careful. Upon his arrival that night, like the last few nights, he'd sent Faith a text telling her that he was in the very last row to the far right of the entrance.

Rather than exit the car, Jerry rolled down the driver's side window and stayed put. It was a warm night with a gentle breeze blowing around. The powerful engines of semis entering and leaving the lot made a continuous, tired roar. Now and then, an employee of the Pilot station announced through a PA system a number indicating that a shower stall was now available for the tired, hot trucker next in line for it. As Jerry waited, he watched an endless parade of tourists and locals stop at gas pumps or enter or leave the convenience store side of the building. A few entered and left the Denny's.

After a minute, Jerry flipped open his cell phone and tried Fox's number. It rang three times before someone answered. "Hello?" Again, it wasn't Fox's voice. "Hello?" Jerry hung up.

Dammit! He cursed his situation. How could things have gone so bad so fast? Less than a week ago, everything had seemed perfect. He and Jade had brought a healthy son into the world. They were set financially. He had finished illustrating

Issue #2 of his comic book and was ready to self-publish it. He had helped someone in distress find a new life. Now, he was the one in distress, hiding out from a predator who wouldn't stop hunting him until he was found, desperate to take his money, his security, and maybe his life as well as the lives of the people he loved. And an important ally, Jack Fox, was suddenly and inexplicably AWOL.

With a sigh, Jerry scanned the parking lot, alert to a threat or anything suspicious. After a moment, he spotted a car, a dark, late model Ford Fusion parked in the second row of spots close to the Denny's entrance. *Could be a rental,* Jerry thought. He also noted two shadowy figures occupying the driver's and passenger's seats. After watching them for a time, Jerry decided that, like him, they were watching the entrance of the restaurant. He concluded that one of those guys in the car was Pete Sharkey. Somehow, he had found Faith. Somehow, her grandmother had revealed that she was working at this Denny's. There was no denying what Fox had told him. This Sharkey fellow was damned good at finding people.

Thankfully, because of Fox, Jerry still he had the upper hand. He opened his phone and called Faith.

Chapter Seventeen
Found

Faith answered after the second ring and said, "Yeah, Jerry? I'll be right out. I'm washing up."

"Don't leave," he said. "They're out here."

"Who?"

"The people after us. They're parked near the entrance. As soon as you come out, you'll lead them to me, and then they'll pounce." Jerry took a breath and thought for a time. "You need to leave by the back entrance. Okay?"

"Yeah, sure." She sighed. "Jerry, I'm scared."

"Yeah, me, too."

"But if they know I work here, they'll find me eventually. I mean, I used my real name, social security number."

"I know. But they still don't know where you're staying, or where Jade and I live."

"But I had to give an address, on the job application." She

seemed close to terms. "I had to give them yours. I...I told Jade, I think."

"That's alright," Jerry said after a moment. "I don't think Denny's would just give that out. Anyway, we'll worry about that later. For now, we got this, getting out of here. We need to escape." After a deep sigh, he said, "Alright. Like I said, meet me at the back entrance. I'm driving over there right now."

Jerry started the car and slowly drove toward the back of the restaurant. It was pitch dark in the small alley between a wall and a green dumpster leading a few feet out from the back entrance. Jerry pulled the car to the end of it and waited. Moments later, Faith walked out, and with her head hunched down, she hurried to the car. But due to his innate predator's intuition, honed by years as a U.S. Marshal, Sharkey had sensed something was up. At five minutes after ten, with Faith having not yet exited the restaurant by the front door, he'd surmised that she'd been tipped off somehow as to his presence and was leaving by the back door.

Jerry pressed a button to roll down the passenger side window as Sharkey's car slowly approached. "C'mon, Faith, get in," he called out as she strode within feet of his car.

A moment later, she had slid into the passenger seat and shut the door. Out of breath, scared, she whispered, "I'm sorry, Jerry."

"I know," he said, and floored it. He swung around with his tires squealing as he headed out of the lot, almost clipping the front bumper of the cab of a semi, before reaching the exit. With a glance left, he pulled north on US 27 causing an oncoming car in the entrance lane to brake hard and blow his horn. By the time Sharkey had figured his intuition had once again been spot on, Jerry had already driven past him and pulled north onto US 27. With a curse, Sharkey gunned it and followed. A few moments after entering US 27, he let out a sigh as he spotted Jerry's car speeding several lengths ahead of him.

Jerry lucked out by making a series of lights through Haines City on his way to Davenport and the entrance onto I-4. Sharkey managed to stay with him by going through two red lights. At the intersection with the entrance road to an outdoor mall, known as Posner Park, Jerry was forced to stop behind a line of cars in the right lane. Glancing up into the rearview mirror, he saw that Sharkey's Fusion had crept within three or four car lengths behind him in the middle lane, its occupants shadowed in the darkness. Suddenly, the guy in the passenger seat exited and ran up between the idling cars.

"Shit," Jerry spat under his breath as the guy wound his way up to the car. Seeing Jerry's concern, Faith turned and looked back and made a mewing sound. "C'mon," Jerry pleaded, and as if on cue, just as the guy had reached his door and pounded on the glass with something metallic that Jerry supposed was a pistol, the light changed. Jerry drove off with the line of cars leaving the guy standing there. Glancing back, he saw him get back into the passenger side of the Fusion.

The entrance to the I-4 was only a tenth of a mile ahead, and the flow of traffic thankfully sped up to it. The Fusion stayed with him and turned onto the I-4 entrance mere seconds after Jerry. The I-4 was busy but not bumper to bumper at this time of night. Once on it, Jerry hoped that he'd be able to get into the left lane and gain some separation from the Fusion. He started figuring a good place to exit, somewhere he could lose Sharkey and his helper.

Finally, he merged onto the interstate, but the Fusion was right with him, no more than a couple car lengths back. Sharkey seemed to be biding his time. "Dammit!" Jerry cursed under his breath as he kept looking up into the rearview mirror. "Dammit!"

"I'm so sorry, Jerry," Faith whispered.

There was nothing else to do but keep on driving and hope for a miracle.

"Dammit," Jerry whispered again as he sped on at eighty, eighty-five miles per hour. He was angry with himself for letting this happen, for letting himself get caught, for so easily giving away the upper hand. He was angry that it was looking more and more like the Anonymous Man at long last had been found.

Part Two
Found

Chapter Eighteen
Lost

"You lost him? He got away?" Jeff Flaherty rolled his eyes and stared up at the ceiling as he leaned back and shook his head. After a few moments, he sat forward and glared at Pete Sharkey sitting with a smirk behind his desk. "You got to be kidding me."

"No, I'm not kidding you," Sharkey snapped. Jeff and Holly were in Sharkey's office on Walden Avenue on a dark, gloomy morning in late October, two days after Sharkey had lost Jerry Shaw and Faith Smith somewhere on Interstate 4 heading toward Orlando. "He got fucking lucky. Drove like a maniac and I got cut-off by a semi. Took an exit or something. I don't know. Anyway, I fucking lost him. Right. Shit happens in the people finding business."

"That's it? Shit happens?"

"No, that's not it," Sharkey said. "We found him. We know

where he's at. I kept two of my guys down there, still looking." He sighed. "Somehow he got tipped off. Not sure how. But I know now, he's no dummy. It's gonna be a challenge catching him."

"He's probably taken his whores and moved across the country by now," Jeff said. "Or out of the country. Could be anywhere. The Anonymous Man remains anonymous. With our money."

Sharkey leaned forward, and his jaw tightened. He didn't need to be told by Jeff Flaherty that the case had taken a bad turn. Once the prey escapes a trap, it's doubly hard to trap it again. But there was no use crying over spilled milk, as they say. This was the time to pick up the pieces, start fresh, and be inspired anew by the chase. What Sharkey needed was to get lucky, for something unforeseen to fall into his lap.

"What the fuck was that Global investigator doing down there?" Jeff asked. "Fox. In Binghamton? Did you figure that out yet?"

"I have no idea," Sharkey admitted. "I was hoping you would."

"I thought he retired," Holly said with a glance at Jeff. "After our trials."

"Maybe Global lured him out of retirement, for this case," Sharkey suggested. "Hired him to follow you two around and see if you'd lead him to the rest of their money. That took him to me, and he followed me to Binghamton."

Jeff considered that scenario for a time. "He still in the hospital?"

With a nod, Sharkey replied, "Yep. And he's gonna be there for a while. He was hurt bad. Bad concussion, broken arm."

"He still down there?"

"No, he's up here, at Buffalo General."

"So some mugger got him?" Jeff asked.

"Looks that way," Sharkey said. He sighed and added, "Like I told you, I saw the whole thing. But even before he got mugged, or whatever, I had noticed him on my tail as I left Julio Gonzalez's house. He stayed with me from there to interview Faith's grandmother; and, even after that, when I stopped at the Denny's for dinner on Vestal Parkway." He shook his head and gave a short laugh. "A fucking Denny's. Anyway, he sat in the parking lot waiting for me to finish." Sharkey laughed again. "And I sat and let him wait. Then, around seven, I scooted back to the hotel. He followed me into the lot and parked, and watched me walk into the lobby, probably thinking I was done for the night and he'd have to start up in the morning, see what I was up to. He'd probably have gone and interviewed Julio Gonzalez and Faith's grandma and see what they told me if the mugger hadn't intervened."

"If he only knew," Holly said. "That Jerry really is alive."

"Yeah, wouldn't that be a shock?" Sharkey replied. He leaned back and continued, "Anyway, after a couple minutes sitting in the lobby, I took a side door and circled around into the lot, hiding behind some cars until I spotted him a couple rows up, as suspected, sitting there, waiting. Then, the dumb shit got out of his car. He's an old man, in his sixties. Looks out of shape.

"And that's when it happened," Sharkey went on. "This shadow of a guy came out of nowhere. He must have been crouching down between some cars nearby. Bald guy, slim. He used something to hit Fox on the side of the head once, then twice. Fox never saw what hit him. He didn't make a sound, just fell sideways in a lump next to his car. It took all of two seconds. As the mugger was sifting through his pockets, some good Samaritan passing by who'd seen the mugging came running and screaming, and the mugger ran off.

"By the time I came over, the Samaritan was kneeling at Fox's side. Fox was a mess, with blood oozing from the top of his head. I took charge, told the Samaritan I was a former cop. The guy nodded, listened. I got him to use his cell and call 911, and told him to go inside the lobby and get some towels, some help. As he did that, I checked for Fox's cell phone, wallet. They were gone."

"The mugger took them," Holly said.

Sharkey ignored her as he continued, "I still had time to get into Fox's car. I reached into his glove compartment and found an insurance card with his name on it. Naturally, he was insured with Global. After that, with the police and an ambulance on their way, I got out of there, not wanting to get caught up as a witness or anything.

"Back in my room, I checked out who this John T. Fox was. That's how I found the Global connection."

"So Global hired him to follow us," Jeff said, "and that led him to follow you to Binghamton, where he almost got killed by a mugger."

"That's the story, so far as I can tell."

"Well, at least Global's off our butts for the time being," Jeff said.

"They probably already assigned someone else to take his place," Sharkey suggested. "But that's the least of our worries."

Chapter Nineteen
Chuck Bruno

At ten that same morning, Chuck Bruno entered Jack Fox's room on the fifth floor of the Buffalo General Hospital. Bruno was in his late forties, of average height with narrow-set eyes set in a perpetual, unhappy frown. He shaved his head, explaining to Fox while they both worked at Global, that it made him look tougher, someone not to be messed with.

Fox had been napping when Bruno walked in, but after Bruno forced out a cough, Fox stirred and stared groggily at his visitor.

"Hiya, Foxy. How ya doin'?"

Jack turned to him. His face was bloated, and there was an ugly, purplish bruise along the left side of his face. His left arm was in a sling as one of the blows had shattered his collarbone. Fortunately, he had not sustained a fractured skull in the attack, but one nasty concussion had left him confused and headachy.

He was also lucky that due to the intervention of a passerby, the mugger had been unable to get off another blow that might have killed him.

"How'm I doin'?" Jack could barely talk above a whisper. His head still throbbed as he turned a bit to get a better look at Bruno. "How's it look like I'm doing?"

"Not so good," Bruno said.

Fox sighed. There was nothing to add. He watched as Bruno backed up from the bed and brushed momentarily against the long curtains on the window as he peeked down at the drab roof of the building next over. After a moment, he turned and sat down on a wide chair at the side of the bed. After crossing his legs and leaning forward, he said, "The Chief sends his regards. And like me, he was wondering what you were doing in Binghamton getting mugged?"

Fox frowned and, after a moment, asked, "Why's that matter to him, or you?"

Fox was not particularly fond of Bruno. They had worked together for only a few months after Bruno had come over from the Philly PD. Though he and Bruno had been in different precincts over their years in the Department, Fox knew from his sources that Bruno had a dark reputation. He was considered somewhat rogue, resorting to questionable tactics in making his arrests. Fox had mentioned this to Chief Reynolds, head of the Special Frauds Unit over at Global, but Reynolds had merely nodded. Someone higher up the Global food chain wanted him added as an investigator, he'd told Fox, and that was that.

"Well, it matters," Bruno said as he leaned back in the chair, "because we thought that you getting mugged there might have something to do with the Jerry Shaw case."

Fox's frown narrowed as he asked, "How so?"

"Well, because an investigator Jeff Flaherty and Holly Shaw hired went down there," Bruno said. "Name of Pete Sharkey, former U. S. Marshal. Not sure why they need an investigator to find their own money. It's curious."

"How do you know that, Chuck?" Fox asked. "That they hired Sharkey, and that Sharkey was down in Binghamton."

"Because I followed him down there," Bruno replied. "And I was in the parking lot of the Holiday Inn where he was staying, following him when you got mugged."

"You saw me get mugged?"

"Sorry to say," Bruno said. "From the other side of the lot. I'd come back to the hotel after following Sharkey all day. Curious, who he saw that day. One Julio Gonzalez, and one Sylvia Dinardo. Not sure what they have to do with our friend, Jerry Shaw, or Holly Shaw and Jeff Flaherty for that matter."

"Maybe they don't have anything to do with them," Fox wheezed, drew in a breath, and added, "maybe Sharkey was there on another case."

"Maybe," Bruno said. "But that still leaves open what you were doing there, following him."

"You see me following him?"

"No, I didn't," Bruno said. "But you got another reason for being in Binghamton, in the very parking lot of the very Holiday Inn Express where Pete Sharkey was staying?"

Fox tried to think, but his head hurt. Still, he decided he had to tell Bruno, and through him, Chief Reynolds, something.

"I was freelancing," he finally blurted, trying to sound convincing. He took a breath and continued, "I thought Sharkey might lead me to the money. Be a bigger take for me that way, if I found it through him, a lot more than the hourly slave wage I'd get if I'd agreed to get put back on the Global payroll." He smiled, but it was brief, and it hurt. "Like what you're making."

After a time, Bruno nodded as if he was buying what Fox was telling him. He uncrossed his legs, leaned forward with his elbows on his knees, and laughed to himself. "Freelancing," he said. "Doesn't sound like you, Foxy. That's not the guy I came to know at Global. You breaking bad in your old age?"

"No," Fox said, and again the smile he tried to give hurt. "Breaking smart."

Suddenly, Bruno turned serious as he stood and glared down at Fox. "Don't fuck with me, Foxy," he said.

"I'm not..."

At that moment, Jerry Shaw walked into the room.

Still glaring, Bruno looked over at him. Jerry nodded to him and turned to Fox on the bed.

"Hi, Uncle Jack," Jerry said. "How ya doin'?"

Chapter Twenty
Uncle Jack

Bruno didn't stay long after Jerry walked in. Fox introduced him to Jerry, they shook hands, and Bruno said he had to get going. He had work to do. Before leaving, he turned to Fox and said, "Well, I guess you won't be freelancing too much in the immediate future, hey, Foxy?"

"Guess not, Chuck," Foxy said with a cross stare.

"Well, see ya," Bruno said. He smiled and nodded to Jerry and walked past him out the door.

As Jerry edged closer to Fox's bed, he asked, "Who was that?"

"Chuck Bruno," Fox said. "Asshole who took over the Jerry Shaw case for Global," he added. "He's been assigned to watch Jeff and Holly." Fox regarded Jerry a moment and commented, "Well, looks like you kept your weight down."

Jerry thought a moment, shrugged and said, "Yeah, the

Anonymous Man has to stay fit. Can't start looking like the old Jerry Shaw. As for you, you look terrible."

"I feel terrible." He wheezed and added, "My doctor tells me I'm lucky to look this good."

"You worked with him there, at Global, Bruno?"

"Few months," Fox said. "But he didn't come here to pay his respects. He came fishing for what I was doing down in Binghamton."

"Getting mugged," Jerry said with a smile.

"Yeah, funny." Suddenly, Fox nodded to the door. "Look, go over and lock the door. If a nurse comes, let her knock." After Jerry had done that and had returned to the bed, in a low, conspiratorial whisper, Fox added, "Chuck Bruno was a bad cop from what I hear. He put in his twenty years on the Philly PD, then suddenly put in his retirement papers. Right after that, he came over to Global. I'm not sure of all the details, why he left the force, or who he knew to get him in at Global. Doesn't matter. What matters is he's a shifty, nasty son-of-a-bitch who smells a rat—me." Fox wheezed and coughed for a time.

"Whoa! Take it easy, Mister Fox. You need a nurse?"

Fox shook his head, turned his head sideways, coughed again, and drew in a breath.

"I'm okay," he said, though he didn't sound or look it. After a moment, he continued, "Anyway, when the Chief couldn't get me back on the case to see what your pals, Holly and Jeff, were up to after their release from prison, he assigned Bruno. And Bruno was in Binghamton following Sharkey, same as me. In fact, he says he saw me get bushwhacked in the parking lot of the Holiday Inn."

"Really?"

"Yeah. Leaves me wondering."

"Wondering what?"

Fox seemed to be mulling something for a time, then shook his head. "Nothing," he said. "Doesn't matter."

"So what did you tell Bruno about why you were down there, in Binghamton?"

"Freelancing," Fox said. "You know, that I was doing the work for myself, as an independent contractor. If I found the rest of Global's money through Sharkey's work, it would mean a better payday than being back as a Global flunkey earning an hourly wage."

"He buy that?"

Fox shrugged and said, "What else can he buy? That I was working for you, the dead insured? Global hasn't figured that out yet. They never bought what Flaherty and Holly told the police; that your death was faked and they didn't kill you."

In the next moment, Jerry's cell phone rang. He frowned, noting the number of the caller on the screen: Fox's number. After a moment, he clicked the answer button and said, "Hello." When no one spoke, he asked, "Who *is* this?"

"Who's this?" said the voice.

Jerry clicked the end-call button and looked up at Fox.

In the parking lot of the hospital five floors below, Chuck Bruno frowned when the guy answering the call he had just placed from Fox's cell phone hung up on him. "Shit," Bruno whispered to himself.

"Who was that?" Fox asked Jerry.

"You." When Fox frowned, Jerry added, "Well, the guy who mugged you, I guess, and took your phone. Can't you track it, where it is, if he's still using it?"

"I tried that, believe me," Fox said. "The guy's slick. He's done what he needs to do to avoid tracking. It's possible to block it if you know what you're doing. Apparently, that guy, the mugger, or whomever, does."

"So, he's got all your contact numbers, including mine."

"Right, that he does." Fox sighed. "You're under Anonymous."

Jerry looked at his phone, sighed, and said, "I think it's time for a new phone."

"So, you gonna tell me what you're doing here? I take it this isn't a social visit."

"Sharkey found me," Jerry said. "Couple nights ago."

Fox tensed up, winced.

"But then he lost me again," Jerry said, and Fox nodded.

Jerry gave him a short version of recent events involving Sharkey down in Florida. Bottom line, Sharkey had found him, and by bad luck, lost him. Jade and the baby and Faith were safe, for the time being, anyway, in a hotel somewhere in Orlando.

"You don't want to tell me which one?" Fox wheezed.

"I'm being extra careful."

"As you should be," Fox said. "I'm sure he's got a couple guys sniffing around down there."

After another sigh, Jerry stepped back and sat in the same chair that Chuck Bruno had vacated only minutes ago, and closed his eyes.

"You looked tired," Fox noted.

Jerry looked at Fox and nodded. "Drove straight through," he said. "Haven't slept in a bit."

"How do you think he found you?" Fox asked.

"Must have been through the sniffing around you saw him do in Binghamton. Through Faith's grandmother is my best guess. Faith said she sent her a letter a few weeks back, mentioned her job at the Denny's."

"That's it then," Fox said. "The letter. The mention of the Denny's and the postmark on the envelope enabled Sharkey to narrow it down to the Denny's where she actually worked."

"Like you mentioned," Jerry said, "that guy is good at finding people." He frowned, and added, "Well, none of that matters now. He found me—they found me, Holly and Jeff— and that's all we need to know. That, and how to get rid of them. Keep them off my rear-end, permanently."

"You got a plan for that?" Fox asked. "Getting rid of them."

With a nod, Jerry said, "Yeah, maybe I do. Something I thought up during the twenty-hour ride up here."

Frowning, Fox asked, "Well, what is it? What's your plan?"

"My specialty," Jerry said. "Setting them up for a classic, fake double-double-cross."

Chapter Twenty-One
A Classic Fake Double-Double Cross

"Okay," Fox said after a moment. "How's it work? Your classic fake double-double-cross?"

"First," Jerry began, "we set up Marshal Sharkey to think you've decided to help him find me—and, of course, get my money, which you'd share with him. You tell him you know that I'm alive, and better yet, that I trust you."

"Okay, that's a start. I'm getting it."

"And that's what you were doing in Binghamton," Jerry went on. "Following him to make sure he didn't find me first. But your little bump on the head has made you figure out that you're going to need help in not only finding me but in making me hand over the money."

"Still with you. Continue."

"You tell him you'll lure me into a trap. You know I'm coming up here, to see what Holly and Jeff are up to. So, once

I get here, you'll find out where I'm staying and tell Sharkey. All Marshal Sharkey has to do is kidnap me up here, contact Jade and ask for the rest of the Global money as a ransom. She'll have no other choice than to turn over the money, which you and Marshall Sharkey get to split fifty-fifty, cutting out Jeff and Holly in the process."

Fox mulled the plan over for a time. Finally, with a frown, he said, "Okay, I get all that. But I'm still not seeing how this gets Sharkey out of your life, or Holly and Jeff for that matter."

"Well, that part of the plan doesn't," Jerry explained. "But the second part does."

Fox closed his eyes. It was getting late in the morning, and his head was starting to hurt. All this talking and listening and concentrating on a complex plan had increased his stress level.

"Okay, go ahead, I'm listening," Fox told Jerry after a moment with his eyes still closed.

"First, as to Jeff and Holly," Jerry said. "I meet up with them and…"

"You what?" Fox suddenly sat up, groaned from the pain from doing that and looked Jerry over with a quizzical frown. "You what?"

"I meet up with Jeff and Holly, tell them I overheard that Sharkey was planning to double-cross them. With you. I say I heard you and Sharkey planning it, the double-cross. Only it's fake, of course, a fake double-cross."

"Okay."

"I tell them I know about Sharkey through my hiring you and after almost being caught by him, I decided the hell with it, I'm tired of running. So, I've come to them to work a deal to split the remaining Global money three ways, since it's only fair anyway.

"During our talk, I also tell Jeff and Holly that Sharkey somehow knows about the body guy, that Jeff killed him. And in the process of bringing that up, I hope that Jeff will admit doing it. Naturally, I'd record all that, my conversations with them." Jerry frowned, sat forward and looked at Fox. "You getting this, Mister Fox?"

Fox nodded and seemed to be considering what Jerry had just told him. Finally, he looked down at Jerry sitting at the side of his bed and said, "Yes, I think so. You get Jeff to admit killing Willie Robinson on tape, and then, at some point, you turn it over to the cops." He frowned and asked, "Okay, that gets you Jeff for murder, and Holly as an accomplice in that, but how do we get Sharkey for anything?"

"On a kidnapping charge," Jerry suggested. "You set up a sting with the police. Tell them that Sharkey has planned my kidnapping."

Fox thought a moment, suddenly nodded and said, "Dan Miller."

"Who?"

"I think I can get Dan Miller involved in that," Fox said. "He's a senior investigator with the State Police. He worked on your case with me, the case that brought down Jeff and Holly. I'm sure he'd be glad to bring them down again, together with a big-time, sleazy private investigator like Pete Sharkey." He thought another moment, and added, "I tell him what's been set up—that Sharkey is going to break into a room and kidnap someone…"

"The Stadium Inn," Jerry finally said. "Room 121. That's where I'm staying."

"Okay, there," Fox said. "He gets a team out there, from the state police's Special Operations Resource Team—SORT, and once they see Sharkey break in, they jump into action and arrest him for attempted kidnapping, and attempted extortion. Two pretty serious felonies. Then, you hand over the tape of Jeff's admissions about killing Willie Robinson, and they go arrest him and Holly for murder."

"That's it," Jerry agreed. "A perfectly executed fake double-double cross."

"Only one problem with it," Fox added.

Jerry nodded and said, "I know. They'd also have to arrest me."

"And, that," Fox added with a sad expression, "would be the end of the Anonymous Man."

Chapter Twenty-Two
Marshal Sharkey

Someone jiggled the handle of the door to Fox's room. After a few moments of rattling, someone knocked.

"Mister Fox?" a man's voice called out.

Jerry's heart raced as he looked down at Fox and whispered, "Who is it?"

With a brief shrug, Fox mouthed, *I have no idea.* In the next moment, he pointed to the closet near the front door. *Hide. In there.*

Jerry grimaced, remembering the last time he had hidden in a closet, but he hurried over and entered the small, cramped space and closed the door. He leaned against the far wall. In front of him hung a bathrobe, a shirt, and a pair of trousers.

"Mister Fox!" The man at the door called again. "Are you alright?"

The visitor fell silent after that, but moments later, there was more jiggling of the handle. Someone was using a key to unlock the door. A heavy-set nurse walked in and hurried around the far side of the bed. Walking behind her was Pete Sharkey. He took the right side of the bed across from the nurse.

Jerry held his breath in the closet as the nurse said, "He's asleep." The nurse went about examining the medical instruments monitoring Fox's condition and the flow of various medicines and pain-killers through intravenous lines. Finally, she turned to Sharkey and said, "His vitals are fine." She looked down at Fox and said, "Mister Fox, you alright? Mister Fox?"

Fox opened his eyes, nodded half-heartedly and whispered, "Tired. Sleep."

"Yes, sleep," the nurse said. "You need to sleep. You've had too many visitors this morning."

"Visitors?" Sharkey asked her.

"Yes, two," she said. "Looks like they wore him out."

Sharkey looked down at Fox and said in a strong, clear voice, "Mister Fox. My name's Pete Sharkey. I'm a private investigator. I have some questions..."

"Didn't you hear him?" asked the nurse with some annoyance. "He's tired. He needs his rest."

Fox turned to Sharkey. He grabbed his left hand and wheezed, "Tomorrow. Come back, first thing. Eight o'clock."

From inside the closet, Jerry heard that and smiled. *Clever ruse, Jack Fox*, he thought. *Clever ruse.*

"You want me to come back at eight tomorrow morning?"

"Yes," Fox whispered as he looked up at Sharkey, his eyes fluttering, feigning that he was about to pass out. "First thing. Eight o'clock. We...we need to talk."

"Look," interrupted the nurse. "He's had enough

excitement this morning. I need him to get some rest. Sorry, but as he said, you'll have to come back tomorrow."

Sharkey stood there a moment, then forcibly nodded and said, "Alright. Tomorrow."

He started away from the bed with the nurse right behind him. On the way out, he suddenly stopped at the closet door and stared at it a moment as if using x-ray vision to peer inside. Jerry tensed, leaned back against the far wall, and held his breath. For a moment, Sharkey appeared ready to reach for the handle and open the door, check what was inside. But the nurse had placed her chubby hand on Sharkey's shoulder. As she applied a small measure of force, Sharkey glanced back at her with a scowl.

"Sir, he needs his rest," the nurse said.

Finally, Sharkey nodded, gave one last look at the closet door, and walked out of the room.

Chapter Twenty-Three
Partners In Crime

By 7:45 the following morning, Jerry had taken a seat in the small waiting room on Fox's floor, down the hall from the nurse's station. From his seat, he had a clear view of the foyer leading from two elevators that came up from the lobby. At 7:55, he tensed when he saw Sharkey exit from one of them. After Sharkey had strolled past the waiting room, Jerry got up and peeked around the door frame and watched as he walked past the nurse's station and down a short hallway until he entered Fox's room.

Fox was up as Sharkey walked in, with his bed inclined upward, so he was sitting up. On his left wrist, Fox wore a Chronograph wristwatch recorder that Jerry had brought him yesterday afternoon from home. Fox had called his wife, Betty, and told her that a young man would be stopping by to pick up the watch that was in the middle drawer of the desk in his den.

Betty didn't ask questions why the "young man" needed it. Over the years, she had learned to stay out of her husband's investigations.

"You're looking much better today, Mister Fox," Sharkey commented as he approached Fox's bed.

"Yeah, I'm feeling better, too, Mister Sharkey," Fox said. That was true. He was feeling better, finally starting to feel like he was on the road to recovery. His head didn't hurt, and he wasn't all that tired after a good night's sleep. "How can I help you?"

"You can start off by telling me what you were doing in Binghamton."

"Same thing you were doing, Mister Sharkey," Fox said. "Trying to find Jerry Shaw."

Sharkey frowned and paused a moment, then said, "Jerry Shaw's dead."

"No, he's not. And we both know that. Only, from what I understand happened to you down in Florida, he might just as well be."

"What do you mean?"

"I mean, I know you found Jerry Shaw down there," Fox explained, "only to lose him again."

"And how would you know that, Mister Fox."

"Jack, call me Jack."

"Jack. How would you know what happened down in Florida between me and Jerry Shaw?"

"Because Jerry called me and told me what happened," Fox said. "That you caught him picking up Faith Smith at a Denny's down there, chased him onto the I-4, only to lose him when a semi got in your way."

Sharkey drew in a breath. This was not what he'd expected.

The script for this meeting was suddenly useless. Finally, he asked, "And why would he tell you something like that?"

"Good question," Fox said. He worried suddenly that the recorder watch was getting all this. "He trusts me, he says."

"Why would he trust you?"

"Another good question," Fox replied. "Why? Because a year ago, I could have nabbed him. Yeah, that's right. It was when I was still working for Global. I figured the whole thing out and had a hunch that he'd be compelled to visit his gravestone on his birthday, September twenty-third. So, I staked it out—the Shaw family plot. And my hunch proved right. As expected, Jerry showed up around eleven, parked his car along the shoulder and trudged his way across the section to the headstone; and, as he was standing there, saying his prayers, I guess, I snuck up behind him, called out his name." Fox laughed. "Scared the bejesus out of him."

"But you let him go. Why would you do that?"

"You know," Fox told Sharkey with a shrug. "I've never quite figured that out." Now that, at least, was true. What had made him do it had never been clear to him. Bottom line, he never thought of Jerry Shaw, aka The Anonymous Man, as a bad guy. And when he thought about it—and he often did—he decided that it would have been like capturing Batman, the Green Lantern, Robin Hood, or any other superhero and ending their superhero careers. "To this day, I can't quite figure it out."

"And why exactly did he call you now?" Sharkey asked. "What does he want?"

"For me to follow his wife, Holly, and Jeff Flaherty," Fox said. "See what they're up to. And, mostly, to watch you."

"Why are you telling me this?"

"Because Jerry made a mistake trusting me," Fox said. He hoped that he sounded convincing, that he could relay a proper motive for making this revelation, for partnering up with Sharkey, after having let Jerry go a year ago. "Because I have no intention of helping him this time. I'd rather help myself."

"Help yourself to the money he's sitting on."

"Right," Fox said. "I could use that money. At least, a portion of it. I didn't realize how unprepared I was for retirement. Living off a cop's pension isn't what it's cracked up to be. That's why I moved to this shithole, to Buffalo. Housing is cheap, though the taxes and weather suck."

"You can say that again," Sharkey replied. "But what does that have to do with me?"

"Because I figured, in my current condition," Fox explained, "that I could use a partner. The way I figure it, Jerry Shaw is sitting on a little over a million bucks. And half that is nothing to sneeze at, certainly better than nothing. For both of us."

"And you want to partner up with me."

"Unless you don't want to," Fox said. "I mean, I don't see you being able to find Jerry after your recent trip to Florida. He's the rabbit that got away, you might say. Gonna be extra careful next time around. I highly doubt that there'll be a next time."

Sharkey nodded and said, "You got a point."

"But involving yourself with me," Fox went on, "someone who knows what hole the rabbit ran into, you're on the hunt again."

"So what's your plan for seizing the prey?"

"We, or you, kidnap Jerry," Fox explained. "Then, you convince Jade to give us the money—well, most of it—as ransom. We let her keep a couple hundred grand, to show our good faith. She sends us the rest, and we send her Jerry, still alive. If she resists, we kill him."

"We ask Jade for ransom," Sharkey said. He smiled down at Fox. "You've given this some thought."

"A half-million dollars is a powerful motivator."

After a time, Sharkey suggested, "You realize that they all may have to go."

"Go?"

"Yeah, go," Sharkey said. "They're witnesses. Jerry, Jade. Faith Smith."

This is going better than expected, Fox thought. *Now he's gone beyond kidnapping. He's talking murder.*

"What about your clients?" Fox asked.

Sharkey laughed and said, "Same deal."

"Kill them, too?"

Sharkey nodded, then whispered, "Yeah. Kill them, too."

Chapter Twenty-Four
Sharkey's Fake Double-Cross

It was eight-thirty by the time Jerry saw Pete Sharkey enter an elevator for the ride back down to the lobby. When the door closed, he got up and headed toward Fox's room.

Fox was still sitting in an inclined position as Jerry approached his bed. With a smile, he told Jerry, "Well, he went for it." He held up his left hand and slid off the watch and handed it to Jerry. "Hopefully, it got all of it, every word." He reported the gist of his conversation with Sharkey. "And the best of it," he said, "he mentioned killing Holly and Jeff as his way to get rid of them. That should get them amply motivated to double-cross him."

"He really proposed that? Killing them?"

Fox nodded and said, "Not to mention, you and Jade."

"He's one nasty player. A bad man."

"That he is," Fox agreed. "Dangerous. But now it's our

turn. First, you take the watch and download on your laptop what I recorded and load it onto a flash drive. You know how to do that?"

"Of course I do. I'm a millennial, remember? Unlike you, we don't remember a time when laptops and flash drives didn't exist. I'm surprised an old-timer like you knows this stuff."

"Don't get smart," Fox said with a wink. "You wear that same recorder watch during your meeting with Holly and Jeff. Understood?"

Jerry nodded.

"And you need to meet with them soon as possible," Fox said. "I told him I'd need some time to arrange our trap for you. What we finally settled on was for me to call you and tell you that Sharkey had approached me and proposed a deal on behalf of himself and Holly and Jeff, the deal being that if I set you up, I'd get a hundred-grand cut of the money."

"Sharkey's own fake double-cross," Jerry commented.

"Something like that," Fox went on. "I was to tell you that you needed to come on up here so that we could set the trap on them—Sharkey and Holly and Jeff—through tape recordings of them incriminating themselves and through a police sting of Sharkey kidnapping you. Isn't that a howl? He came up with our exact plan."

"And then," Jerry guessed, "when I come up to do that, he and a few of his henchmen nab me in the room I'm staying at and tried to squeeze Jade for the ransom."

"Exactly," Fox said. "Our exact plan, except without the sting. Once he's kidnapped you, he takes your cell, finds Jade's number, calls and tells her unless she sends a million bucks to an account he gives her, you're dead. To give her some incentive to go along with this deal, a measure of good faith on his part, if you will. He tells her she can keep anything over the mil. He didn't want to be greedy."

"Only a hundred grand, give or take a few dollars," Jerry commented. "We got a million point one in the bank. Like I said, give or take a few dollars.

"Yeah, we figured about that much." Fox sighed. "So, that's it. He's gonna lie low until I reach out and tell him it's all set. That you've arrived and where you're staying. I figure that might buy us a day at most. The glitch is the part of his plan to kill Holly and Jeff. I'm not sure when he's going to do that."

"Okay, so I probably have less than a day to get Holly and Jeff to make an admission about the body guy on tape. And get them into a safe space."

"Yes, that's it," Fox agreed. "A day or so at most."

"Alright, better get going then," Jerry said as he looked at the recorder watch now wrapped around his left wrist.

"You know how you're gonna approach them?" Fox asked. "Remember, they're probably being watched by Sharkey, or someone working for him, until he's ready to go kill them. Not to mention Chuck Bruno or someone he hired if he's still watching Sharkey."

"Well, I can't exactly walk up the driveway to their apartment."

"No," Fox agreed. "Unless you really can become invisible."

"You said they live in the upper flat, right?"

"Right. In a place on Colton Avenue in Lackawanna."

"Is the entrance in the back?"

"Yeah," Fox said. "Up one of those enclosed stairwells."

Jerry nodded as he thought for a time. Finally, he asked, "You think it's accessible from the houses on the street parallel to Colton?"

Fox nodded. "Yeah, sure, I think so," he said. "Victory Place, I think it's called."

Jerry thought for a little while, then said, "First, I meet with them somewhere. At some public place." He looked up at Fox. "That supermarket you followed them to."

"The Sav-a-Lot." Fox nodded. "Yes. The one they took a cab to."

"I drive over there this morning, to their apartment. I park and watch them, careful to avoid Sharkey and Bruno or their guys watching them."

Fox nodded again as Jerry went on, "Hopefully, they'll need to do some shopping. Maybe this morning. I follow the cab to the Sav-a-Lot and follow them inside, once again careful to avoid Bruno and Sharkey. Once inside, I run into them. After the initial shock of that meeting wears off, I tell them I have to talk to them about Pete Sharkey, right away, that he's double-crossing them. I'll arrange a little pow-wow for tonight. Come in through the back entrance through the door that they'll leave open for me."

"If they go to the Sav-a-Lot," Fox said doubtfully. "They might go nowhere."

"No, Jeff gets antsy. He'll want to do something. If not the Sav-a-Lot, then the mall. Somewhere. I just have to go there, too. Meet up with them and arrange a meeting for tonight."

"Through the back door, in the darkness."

"Yes," Jerry agreed. "So I can't be seen. Then, I tape our meeting." He held up the watch and said, "With this. And get them out of that apartment, away from Sharkey."

"Unless Sharkey gets to them, first," Fox said. "There's several hours between now and tonight."

"I know," Jerry said. "But I think Sharkey'll see the wisdom of getting my money first, and killing me, before killing them."

Fox nodded and said, "You may have something there."

"Well, better get going," Jerry said.

"Just be careful about Sharkey and Bruno," Fox said and sighed. "One thing I am worried about."

"What's that?"

"What if Sharkey has smelled a rat and figured things out and is double-crossing us?"

Chapter Twenty-Five
Holly and Jeff

By nine-fifteen, Jerry was driving down Colton Avenue in a black Nissan Rogue with Florida plates, registered to Jade, toward the house at 151 Colton where Jeff and Holly lived in the small, upper apartment. Along the way, he passed a car parked on the other side of the street with shadowy guy hunched up behind the steering wheel on the driver's side, waiting for something. He guessed that the guy worked for either Chuck Bruno or Pete Sharkey. It gave Jerry pause that he didn't see two cars with guys staking out 151 Colton, one working for Bruno and the other working for Sharkey.

Still, that the guy in the car was still there, and whether he was working for Bruno or Sharkey, it pleased Jerry. It told him that Holly and Jeff were still in the upper flat and hadn't yet gone anywhere. It also meant that they weren't likely to be dead.

Jerry drove down Colton a few more houses, then turned

around, drove back the other way and parked a few houses down on the same side as the guy already staking out Holly and Jeff. He hunched down and after a time lifted the Kindle that Fox had lent him for the stake-out.

"A stake-out can be boring work," Fox had told him. "Best to have something to read." Fox recommended the novel he'd just finished, *Lawyers Gone Bad*, for that purpose. Not five minutes into it, Jerry saw a cab pull up in front 151 Colton. A minute or so later, Jeff and Holly were hustling down the driveway to the cab. As the cab drove off up Colton, the guy working for Bruno or Sharkey took off as well. A moment later, so did Jerry.

They turned right onto Ridge Road and quickly drove through downtown Lackawanna, a drab section with old, squat buildings. After crossing the intersection with South Park Avenue, the cab went past the seemingly out-of-place Our Lady of Victory Basilica, a beautiful marble replica of one of those gigantic Italian churches from Medieval times. It had been built in the 1920s by the city's patron saint, Nelson Baker, and was where Jerry's fake funeral mass had been held three years ago. They drove past the enormous Holy Cross Cemetery, where Jerry's fake gravestone still stood. Finally, after several more lights, the cab made a left turn onto Abbott Road, then another quick right into the parking lot of the aging Abbott Road Plaza. Along the way, Bruno or Sharkey's man stayed a few car lengths behind the cab, and Jerry remained a few car lengths behind him.

The plaza's stores were housed in an L-shaped building constructed more than seventy-five years ago. A spacious asphalt parking lot spanned out from the stores with only a small portion of the available spaces occupied these days. At one time, the Abbott Road Plaza had been a bustling shopping center. Like much of the area when Lackawanna and South Buffalo were thriving neighborhoods of steelworkers and laborers, it had seen better days. On that morning, the place looked beat-up and tired, like most of its present shoppers.

The Sav-a-Lot grocery market was at the far corner of the L-shaped building next to a cancer foundation thrift shop. Bruno or Sharkey's guy took a random spot with a clear view of the entrance to the market. Jerry parked in the next row, further back. He exited the car and made his way into the store.

The patrons of this Sav-a-Lot were mostly old and poor and certainly ethnic. Many of them were Muslim women who wore the traditional hijab, some with veils leaving only a slit for their eyes.

When Jerry spotted Jeff and Holly in the store, Jeff was leaning forward, looking bored, pushing a cart down the produce aisle along the far-right wall. Holly had picked out a green pepper and dropped it into the cart. In that moment, Jerry marveled how low they had fallen from their cocky days planning his fake death in what had been his and Holly's living room. By then, Jeff had gotten into the habit of berating him about his weight and intelligence and was probably already banging Holly. How things had changed in three years. Now, they blended in with the other Sav-a-Lot shoppers with their worn, old jeans and shabby jackets. Jerry couldn't help but smile and feel a level of satisfaction at how things had turned out. He was a millionaire, an anonymous man, while they had become the dregs of society.

Jerry walked quickly down to the end of the aisle next to theirs and stood back, waiting for them to round the corner. As Jeff pushed forward with Holly looking for some item, Jerry stepped out.

"Wow," Jerry said, "they let anyone shop here."

Jeff stopped the cart and stood straight up. Holly simply gawked at him. It occurred to Jerry that the last time he'd seen him, Jeff tried to choke him to death.

After a time, Holly whispered, "Jerry?"

"At your service," he said. "But I have no time to chit-chat. We need to talk. Your investigator is setting you up—setting *us* up. Maybe it's time to get the team back together." *How ironic that would be*, thought Jerry.

"What're you talking about?" Jeff snapped. He looked around and lowered his voice. "Where's our fucking money?"

Jerry stepped forward and stood before him. "Your fucking money?" he said. "Excuse me? You spent it." Jerry shook his head and looked around, just to be sure nobody was watching, and saw that the few shoppers hadn't appeared to notice them. "Look, you just keep your back door open tonight. Like I said, we need to talk. I'll come over around seven."

Jerry looked around again, turned back to them and smiled. "I don't know how you shop in this shithole." He turned and walked away.

Chapter Twenty-Six
An Honorable Man

After his meeting with Jeff and Holly at the Sav-a-Lot, Jerry drove back toward their upper flat. He passed Colton Avenue and turned left onto Victory Place, the next street over. After finding a similar old, hulking clapboard house on Victory directly behind the two-family house where Holly and Jeff's upper flat was located, Jerry parked and scanned the area. He noted a narrow, bumpy asphalt driveway along the side of the house, with weeds growing through the cracks. He took a chance and walked to the back of the house. The place seemed deserted, with the residents probably working or asleep. Nobody stopped him or seemed to care that he was walking toward the back of the house. A short backyard with a chain-link fence separated the house from the equally short yard at the back of the house where Holly and Jeff lived.

"Perfect," Jerry whispered to himself. Tonight, in the

darkness, he could easily hop the fence and make it unseen, especially from Colton Avenue, to the back door leading up the stairs to Jeff and Holly's flat.

After that, Jerry returned to his room at the Stadium Inn. He powered up his laptop and downloaded Fox's conversation with Sharkey that morning. Everything was clear. The recorder watch had worked to perfection. Next, Jerry downloaded the recording to a flash drive that Fox could give to the police after they had arrested Sharkey for attempting to kidnap him. Jerry tested the recorder watch to make sure he knew how to use it during his visit with Holly and Jeff that evening.

Before stepping out for lunch, Jerry called Fox on the new prepaid cell phone he'd bought the previous night for cash at a Walmart not far from the Stadium Inn.

"It's all set," Jerry said. "I'm meeting them tonight."

"How was the tape of my call?"

"Perfect," Jerry said. "Clear as a bell. Incriminating statements galore."

"Alright, great," Fox said. "I just got off the phone with Dan Miller, from the State Police. It's all set. It's a go. We just need to decide when. Sharkey's gonna get antsy, expecting you to show up here." He sighed. "I was thinking tomorrow night."

Jerry thought about that for a time. Finally, he said, "Alright, tomorrow night. Nine-ish?"

"Yeah, sure," Fox said. "Nine-ish. I didn't give Miller much in the way of details. He wasn't happy about that. Like, for example, I didn't tell him who Sharkey was going to kidnap and hold for ransom."

"Why not? Why didn't you tell him it was me?"

"I want to give you an out," Fox explained. "I want to give you time to think it through. Decide if you really wanted to stop being the Anonymous Man. After it's over, you can probably work a deal with the DA. You'd have helped bring down a bad private investigator and even more than that, helped them put a murderer back in jail. But in exchange, you'd be giving up a lot—a million dollars and your lack of an identity."

Jerry sighed and said, "I know what I'd be giving up. I don't think I have any other choice unless you can come up with one."

"Well, still, I left Miller in the dark as to the victim. As I said, he wasn't happy about it, but he still agreed to help me set up the sting."

Jerry nodded and pondered for a time whether he could truly trust Jack Fox. What if Fox really did need the money, like he had told Sharkey on the tape. If the plan he was suggesting worked, he'd get a fee from Jerry, but only a fraction of what he could be getting if he let Sharkey kidnap him. What if Fox was working with Sharkey and they were planning their own fake double-double cross of him?

But in the next moment, Jerry chose not to believe that. He accepted that Jack Fox was a good and honorable man, intent on obtaining justice. That he'd been an honest cop, honest Global investigator, and now an honest friend.

"Okay," Jerry said at last. "Nine tomorrow night, we fake double-double cross Pete Sharkey and better yet, Holly and Jeff."

Chapter Twenty-Seven
Bingo!

A few minutes before seven, Jerry parked on Victory Place, a few houses down from the house behind the one on Colton Avenue. He hustled along the wall of the house in the darkness, down the bumpy asphalt driveway to the backyard, and without a thought, hopped the fence. A moment later, he opened the door leading up a narrow wooden staircase to the entrance of Holly and Jeff's upper flat.

After reaching the top landing, he drew in a breath and knocked. Jeff opened the door a moment later. With a frown, he stepped back, enabling Jerry to enter a small kitchen with an old white stove and small fridge in one corner next to a Formica countertop. Jeff went over and sat next to Holly at the kitchen table.

Like earlier in the day, Holly looked beat-up, tired. A year in jail and living poor had aged her. For the most part, she could no longer pass for Jade's twin sister. She'd dyed her hair from blonde to brunette and now looked considerably older. Maybe after a few weeks of living better, and dying her hair back to its natural blonde, she'd get back her spark.

After his call to Fox that afternoon, Jerry had called Jade. After she told him that she and the baby and Faith were doing fine, coping, he gave her an update about his meeting with Fox, Fox's meeting with Sharkey, and his upcoming meeting with Holly and Jeff. That worried her. She didn't trust them. They'd try and figure out some way to hurt him.

"You going in armed?"

Jerry said, "No, I don't think there's a need for that. First, they need to hear me out. And once they do, they know they have more to fear from Pete Sharkey than me."

She grunted, unconvinced. "Just be careful." After a sigh, she added, "And don't let Holly get to you."

Jerry groaned and said, "Don't worry about that, about me." And yet, she had a right to be troubled about it after what he'd pulled last time that had almost gotten himself killed. "I know what she is. She's used up all the trust I could ever give her."

After a moment, Jade whispered, "But sometimes I wonder, Jerry."

"Wonder what?"

"That you still love her."

He sighed and rolled his eyes and thought, *here it comes, that old, tired conversation between them.* Instead of joining in the debate, in a confident voice, he said, "Well, you have nothing to wonder about."

She remained silent for a time, then said, "I miss you,

Jerry." After another moment, through some soft sobs, she continued. "But it doesn't look like I'm gonna be seeing you for a while."

Jerry couldn't disagree. Once the fake double-double cross went down, he'd be arrested and would have to bargain for a reduced sentence. Even with a good deal, it was almost certain that he'd be spending some time in prison. He hoped what Fox had told him would come true; that the DA and the judge would be sympathetic considering his help in putting three pretty bad people in prison.

"It'll work out, Jade," Jerry said. "You have to believe that. Once this goes down, and I serve my time, I'll come back to you and the baby, free of Holly and Jeff, and we'll start leading normal lives."

Her crying over, she drew in a breath and said, "Yeah, but the Anonymous Man will be dead."

"Seems like old times," Holly said from across the kitchen table. Jerry looked up and saw her smiling at him. Could it be possible that she was trying to seduce him yet again? In that moment, Jerry felt a ping of regret, a yearning for Holly, proving again that Jade was right to worry, that she saw through his protests that he no longer had any feelings for Holly.

"Yeah, old times," Jeff scoffed. "Now, you wanna tell us what you were talking about this morning, Jerry-boy? That Pete Sharkey's double-crossing us?"

There it was, despite everything that had happened the last three years, that old condescension in Jeff's voice. Jerry turned to him with a scowl. Who was Jeff to feel superior to him at that moment? Jerry was no longer the chubby, useless guy scared of his own shadow. Didn't he know that? Had Jeff forgotten that he'd beaten him, sent him to prison? Of course, Jeff could argue that Jerry had nothing to do with it; that if not for his woman, Jade, coming to the rescue, he'd be a dead man and Jeff would have all of Global's money.

"That's right," Jerry said. "Sharkey's double-crossing you, and even worse, setting you up for murder. With my investigator, Jack Fox."

"Your investigator? Fox?" Jeff asked incredulously. After a time, he nodded and guessed, "So that's why he was in Binghamton. He was working for you."

"Yes, exactly," Jerry said. "He was following Sharkey for me, see what he'd dig up down there that could lead him to me in Florida. Anyway, Sharkey found enough, and almost caught me. But I got lucky and got away."

"Yeah, we heard that," Jeff said. "You got lucky."

"But now I learned that Fox, like Sharkey, is a snake," Jerry continued.

"What are you talking about?"

"See, I found out that Fox got mugged down in Binghamton, hurt pretty bad."

"Yeah, we heard that, too," Jeff said.

"Mister Sharkey told us," Holly added.

"How does that show Fox is a snake."

"I'm getting to that," Jerry said. "See, I came up north once his mugging came to my attention. I needed to find out what Fox had learned before he got mugged. How he might still help me. Plus, I felt responsible for him getting hurt.

"Anyway, when I came to his hospital room yesterday afternoon, he was asleep. And shortly after that, Sharkey arrived. I had just enough time to sneak into the closet."

"That your specialty, Jerry-boy?" Jeff asked with a smirk

that Jerry suddenly wanted to wipe off.

"It does serve a purpose," Jerry replied, glaring at Jeff. "Gets me important information. Like, last time, when I overheard you two assholes planning the murder of Willie Robinson, not to mention mine. This time, I heard Sharkey and Fox plan to double-cross me, and then kill you and Holly."

"What's that?" Jeff asked. "Kill me and Holly?"

Here's my chance, thought Jerry. He had sort of planned it this way, find a way to turn the conversation in such a way that Jeff would admit killing Willie Robinson. Jerry looked at Jeff and asked, "Remember doing that, Jeff? Planning Willie Robinson's murder?" After Jeff shrugged, Jerry probed, "Is that a yes?"

"Yeah, so what?"

"And planning mine? My murder?"

"Yeah, like I said, so what? That's ancient history."

"Well," Jerry said, slowly and carefully, "you got to really pull off your plan for Robinson, but not for me, right?"

"And I'm still asking, so what?" Jeff said.

Jerry wondered if that was enough. Should he raise their suspicions and try for more?

"You gonna get to the point or what?" Jeff asked. "What exactly did you overhear Fox and Sharkey talking about while you were hiding in the closet?"

"Yeah, sure, I'll get to that," Jerry said. "But you should never have done that. Killed him, Willie Robinson. He was our partner. Irks me to this day."

"Our partner? We had no other choice," Jeff said. "The guy was blackmailing us. Wanted more of our fucking money. Plus, he was a fucking drunk. So, I fucking killed him. So, fucking what?"

Jerry looked down at the watch on his left wrist and thought, *Bingo!*

Chapter Twenty-Eight
Self-Defense

"So, why don't you get to what you overheard Fox and Sharkey talking about while you were in that closet, Jerry-boy," Jeff said.

"Look, it's not Jerry boy, it's just plain, Jerry."

Jeff shrugged and said, "Okay, just plain Jerry. What did you hear?"

"What I heard is that Fox is going to give me up to Sharkey," Jerry said. "Tell Sharkey where I'm staying so he can break into the room and kidnap me. Once Sharkey has me, he'll find Jade's number on my cell phone and call her demanding a ransom. The Global money."

"You sure she'd do that, give up the money?" Holly asked. "For you."

"Yes, I'm sure," Jerry said and glared again at Holly. "She loves me."

With a short laugh, Holly asked, "You sure about that?"

"Cut the crap, Holly," Jeff said, glaring at her. He turned back to Jerry. "Go on."

"Once they have the money, or most of it, I'm not sure what they're planning. Let me go, or kill me."

"They'll kill you," Jeff smiled. "I would. Why leave any witnesses? And you're already dead, officially. They'll kill you and get rid of your body, and no one will be the wiser. As for Jade, what can she do, go to the cops, report the stolen money she was in possession of was itself stolen?"

"Well, whatever," Jerry said. "I don't intend to get put in that position. As for you two, Sharkey told Fox, and Fox agreed, that they had no other choice than to kill you both. You know too much about everything, and the way Sharkey put it, he didn't like to leave witnesses. So maybe you're right about their ultimate plans for me as well.

"Plus, like me, you two won't exactly be missed. I mean, if they make you disappear, who'd really care, right? Jeff has no family to speak of, no friends. And your family, Holly, even your brother, Raymond has pretty much given up on you, as far as I understand. Everyone will figure that you two left town to get away from the bad publicity and start over doing whatever."

"You're wrong, Jerry," Holly said. "My family hasn't given up on me. I don't know where you got that. Raymond is letting us use this apartment."

"But if you left town, how hard would anyone, including Raymond, look for you?"

Holly gave a sheepish shrug and looked away.

"Why're you telling us this, Jerry?" Jeff asked. "Why help us? What's in it for you? Why don't you just go back down to your woman in Florida and live happily ever after?"

"I'm helping you to help me," Jerry said. "If I don't, I'll forever be on the run, looking over my shoulder for Sharkey and Fox. So, I figured, I need to bring them down. And to do that, I need to work with you. We need to work together, resurrect our conspiracy."

Holly shot Jerry a look and asked, "Do you have a plan for that? For bringing them down?"

"A plan? Yes." Jerry leaned forward and glared at Jeff. "We have to kill them both. I pretend to fall for Fox's trap, but before Fox and Sharkey get a chance to execute it, Jeff figures out a way to sneak up on Sharkey and, well, kill him. Put a knife in his back somewhere he won't be expecting you, or shoot him in the head. Whatever works."

"A gun," Jeff said. "I think I know where I can get one. What about Fox?"

"Sharkey's not going to be easy," Holly broke in. "He's smart and tough."

"So am I. Smart and tough," Jeff boasted and flashed a smile at Holly. "Plus, he won't be suspecting me. I'll have the element of surprise."

Jeff turned to Jerry and asked, "What about Fox? What do you have in mind for him?"

"Same thing," Jerry said. "Murder. He'll be the easier of the two. Helpless in a hospital room. I'll do that one. I owe it to him."

"You?" Jeff said and smirked. "Can you really do that, kill someone?"

Jerry glared at Jeff and said, "Sure, if they meant to kill me." He relaxed and added, "I figure, I owe it to the old bastard for setting me up. And as I said, it'll be easy. He won't be suspecting me either. I should be able to sneak up there after hours. The nurses are half-asleep anyway. Stick him with a knife or suffocate him at two in the morning, and sneak out again."

After a moment, Jeff asked, "And then what, after we take Sharkey and Fox out? How's your resurrected conspiracy work?" He looked over at Holly. "What's the reward?"

"Like all conspiracies, resurrected or not, an equal split," Jerry said. "We split the insurance money, what's left of it, three ways. That's about four hundred grand each."

"And you'd give that up so easy, eight hundred grand?" Jeff asked.

"Yes, I would," Jerry said. "For peace of mind. It'd be worth it. Four hundred thousand is still a lot of money. The alternative is spending the rest of my days running from Sharkey and Fox and maybe, you and her. And I wouldn't lose any sleep over the deaths of two scumbags like Sharkey and Fox, after what they have in mind for us."

"It's self-defense," Holly said. "Just like with the body guy."

"Yeah," Jerry said, marveling how convincing he'd sounded. "Self-defense."

"Exactly," chimed in Jeff. "Just like Willie Robinson. Self-fucking defense."

Chapter Twenty-Nine
The Set Up

Jerry convinced Holly and Jeff not to stay in their upper flat another minute. He suggested they book a room at a Holiday Inn across the street from the airport and also rent a car.

"Either of you still have a credit card?" Jerry asked. "Obviously, a dead man doesn't."

Both said they did. Using Jeff's card, Jerry called the hotel, booked them a room, and then rented a car in Jeff's name at a rental place near the hotel.

Right after that, they left the same way Jerry had come: out the back door and over the fence into the backyard of the house behind them. They walked down the narrow driveway to Victory Place and into Jerry's waiting car.

It was almost eleven by the time Jerry returned to his motel room. The first thing he did was upload the watch recording into his laptop and then download it onto a flash drive. He listened to the recording and smiled, certain that the several admissions Jeff had made about killing Willie Robinson would put him in prison for life. Holly would get less time as an accomplice, but she'd certainly go to jail as well. A part of him felt bad about Holly doing more time. Jeff had been the real culprit, the evil mastermind, behind Willie Robinson's murder and the plan to murder him. Jeff had corrupted her, for sure, but Jade was right. Holly was a big girl, and she had gone along with Jeff's malicious dealings seemingly without a second thought, and worse, she had orchestrated Jerry's ambush down in Florida.

Whether or not Jerry was upset about Holly's fate didn't matter now. It was out of his control; and, yet, it wasn't. As Fox had noted, he could still back out, return to Florida and lead a life on the run from Holly and Jeff and Sharkey, hoping that at some point down the road, they'd grow tired of chasing an anonymous man who kept one step ahead of them.

No, Jerry finally told himself. A life on the run was no life.

He cleared his mind of all the turmoil broiling through it and listened to the recording of his meeting with Holly and Jeff, scribbling down on a small, motel notepad Jeff's incriminating statements.

He called Jack Fox. As soon as Fox picked up, Jerry said, "It worked."

"You sure?"

"Yes, I'm sure."

Jerry described his meeting with Holly and Jeff and read Jeff's admissions.

"He's toast," Fox agreed. "Good job."

Jerry explained that he'd dropped Holly and Jeff off at the car rental place and drove over with them to the Holiday Inn on Genesee Street across from the airport where they'd booked a room.

"Good, at least they're safe from Sharkey," Fox said. "Now, we have to make sure Jeff doesn't go after Sharkey and somehow get lucky. I want Pete Sharkey in jail, not dead."

"I think Jeff's a ways from pulling that off," Jerry suggested. "First, he has to get a gun. Then he has to watch Sharkey to find a good time to try and take him down. By then, I hope this thing'll be over, and Jeff will be in custody for the Willie Robinson murder. I told Jeff that I wasn't going to be set up for a couple days. He has no idea that it's really going down tomorrow."

"Alright, sounds good," Fox said after a moment. After a sigh, he told Jerry, "Look, I had visitors this afternoon and evening. First, Pete Sharkey, then Chuck Bruno. Luckily, they didn't run into each other."

"Yeah, what did they want?"

"Bruno supposedly to see how I was doing," Fox said. "But he was fishing for information. And Sharkey, to finalize the plan for nabbing you and killing Jeff and Holly. And lucky you got them out of there tonight. He plans on going to their flat either late tonight or first thing tomorrow morning with a couple of his quote, 'associates' to do the deed."

"I figured they needed to get out of there. So, where do we go from here?"

"From here," Fox said, "I set up your kidnapping with Sharkey. I give him your motel room, and he does the rest. Tomorrow night, like we agreed, nine o'clock. And when he nabs you, we nab him. Miller's all set with his men to do just that—a sting, for tomorrow night, with guys from the SORT team. Though he's still not happy, I haven't revealed who Sharkey intends to kidnap.

"After that," Fox went on, "I give Miller the recording you made tonight, and he pays Jeff and Holly a visit at their hotel and arrests them. And that's it, case closed."

"Yeah, case closed," Jerry said with a sigh, his nerves already on edge. "Tomorrow," he said and drew in a breath.

"Yep, tomorrow," Fox said. "You sound nervous. Want to back out?"

"No, I don't. It's just…"

"Look, Miller will have some crack men with him," Fox assured him. "Real pros, like Navy Seal team guys. As soon as Sharkey grabs you, they'll swoop in. End of kidnapping. End of Pete Sharkey."

"And the end of the Anonymous Man."

"Well, yeah, but you knew that going in."

"I know," Jerry said, "but now that it's really happening, I'm having seller's remorse. I'll be sad to see him go. I really like that guy, the Anonymous Man."

"So do I," Fox said and sighed. "Look, I told you before, you still can change your mind. Remember, Miller still doesn't know it's you who Sharkey is going to kidnap. And, if I call it off, there's no way he can make me tell him. There'd be nothing to tell."

But suddenly, Jerry's doubt about Fox crept in. Maybe he wasn't the honest guy he believed him to be.

"Can I trust you, Mister Fox?" Jerry asked.

"Why, don't you?" When Jerry didn't answer right away, Fox repeated, "Don't you?"

"Maybe I'm just getting cold feet" Jerry finally answered.

"Maybe a life on the run wouldn't be such a bad thing after all. I'll have a good head start."

"Well, you just tell me what you want me to do," Fox said. "I haven't told Sharkey where you're staying yet."

Jerry thought for a time. Finally, he blurted out, "No, go ahead, set it up. Tomorrow night the Anonymous Man retires."

Chapter Thirty
Jade

It was close to Midnight by the time Jerry had finished talking to Fox. Though he was worn out after a long couple of days, before getting to sleep, he needed to call Jade.

She answered after the first ring. "How'd it go?" she asked, whispering. "Your meeting with those two?"

Jerry sat against the headboard of the lumpy bed, propped up by three small, too-soft motel pillows. The 19-inch blurry TV set on an old, worn, fake-oak dresser was on, playing one of the late-night shows with the sound turned low.

"It went great," he said. "That asshole, Jeff, confessed everything. That he murdered Willie Robinson. It'll put him and Holly back in jail."

"And you, too."

"Well, Fox agrees I can probably negotiate a decent deal," Jerry said, confident about the outcome. After all, the prosecution like Jeff and Holly for murder wouldn't have happened without him. Not to mention that they'd be able to put a bad investigator, Pete Sharkey, behind bars. "Give back the money, or most of it, and maybe even get off with probation."

"I doubt that," Jade said with a sigh.

"Well, if not probation," Jerry replied, trying to still sound optimistic, "a short prison sentence."

"And, you'll get your life back," Jade added. "Become Jerry Shaw again."

Jerry wasn't so sure that was a good thing, being Jerry Shaw again. It meant losing his persona as the Anonymous Man. But the Anonymous Man would live on in his comic books. Yeah, at least he'd have that, even in prison, working on issues three and beyond, and getting them published in his own name, without having to hide behind the pseudonym, "Anonymous."

"How are you and Seius doing?"

"He's been fussy all day," she said. "Ornery. Asleep now, finally. It's being cramped up in this stuffy room."

"He senses your worry," Jerry added.

"Yeah, that too. But what else can I do?" After a moment, she said, "It's so hard being stuck here. Like his mommy, Seius wants to go home, get back into his crib, stretch out in his own house. I think he senses we are on the run, in danger."

"Can't be helped. You can't go home. Not yet. Sharkey has some of his apes still down there, looking for you." He sighed and asked, "How's Faith holding out?"

"Antsy, like me," Jade said. "She wants out of here, too. But I'm glad to have her. She's been a big help. She's so down, though. You know, she was on the verge of finally getting on with her life, getting out from under the cloak of the

136

Anonymous Man. Breaking free. Now that hope is gone, and she's stuck in limbo. Plus, she feels responsible for messing things up."

"It's not her fault," Jerry said. "Make sure she knows that. And, soon, she'll be breaking free again, once this caper goes down."

"So what's next? What is the caper?"

Jerry sighed again, reluctant to tell her. Finally, he did—how the next night at nine o'clock, Pete Sharkey would break into his room and kidnap him. When he did that, Fox had arranged for the state police to swoop in and arrest Sharkey. And him. And soon after that, the rest would be history. Sharkey would go to jail, lose his PI license, and Jeff and Holly would stand trial again. They'd go to jail again, this time for a murder they actually did commit.

"I don't like it, Jerry," Jade said after a time.

"What don't you like?"

"You trust Fox?"

"Yes," Jerry said but didn't mention his worry about Fox in the back of his mind. "He could have had me a long time ago."

"But maybe he regrets not having turned you in," Jade said. "And this is a way for him to make up for that, and make some money in the process."

"You need to start trusting people," Jerry said with a brief laugh.

"And you need to start not trusting them," she replied. "You know why? Because most people can't be trusted."

"Well, I trust Fox." He sighed. "I...I have to. I need him to solve this problem of always being on the run from Holly and Jeff and Pete Sharkey."

"And how's it with Holly?" she asked. "How'd that go?"

"What do you mean, how'd that go? It went fine. I told you, I don't have any feelings for her."

"But you did once."

"That was before she became who she is," Jerry said, regretting where this was going, the start of that sad, stale argument. *You brought her down to Florida,* Jade invariably would toss in his face somewhere during it, like a bucket of ice water. *You almost got yourself killed.* And his response, invariably, *I learned from that. I learned what she really is.* And finally, her: *Why did you have to learn anything?* Which he never answered. *Maybe because she still looks so much like you,* Jerry thought, but never said. *Maybe because once you love somebody, you never stop.*

"She still batting her eyes at you, trying to tempt you?"

"Stop it," he said. "And no, she looks like what she's become, a skank. Jeff's skank."

That ended it, for now.

"I'm coming up there," Jade suddenly said.

"Coming up here? Absolutely not!"

"You need me."

"Our son needs you," he said. "I told you, it's all set. By this time tomorrow, Sharkey and Holly and Jeff will be toast, in custody, going to prison." When Jade didn't respond to that, Jerry said, "Don't Jade. Please don't. It's gonna work out. I told you. I'm handling it. You come up here, you could ruin things."

Like last time? Jade thought, but didn't say it. Last time, when he almost got himself killed, and she had to come save him.

Chapter Thirty-One
Holly

After the call with Jade, despite how tired he was, Jerry couldn't fall asleep. He tossed and turned, thinking about tomorrow night, wondering if he should really trust Jack Fox, worried about all the things that could go wrong. He had a child to care for, not to mention Jade, and in less than twenty-four hours all that would be placed in serious jeopardy. He'd probably lose his freedom and all his property, not to mention the possibility of losing his life.

At some point, he finally managed to fall asleep. He woke a couple hours later, got out of bed and trudged into the bathroom, peed. Back in bed, he had a hard time falling asleep again, still tormented by his concerns. Maybe he should take his chances and run. Figure out how to get a new identity and resume his life under it. Escape everything, go overseas. Some people did that after some earlier mishap in their lives, forever hiding out. He wondered if the worry ever stopped haunting them. And in his case, he'd have a trained fugitive hunter on his trail driven by the promise of all that money at the end of the hunt.

Jerry was troubled, too, that despite his promise to Jade, Holly kept popping into his head. She may not have looked her best after spending a year in prison and living a hobo's life with Jeff, but she was still his wife, a woman he had known for over ten years. A woman he had once loved, deeply. A woman who still turned him on despite everything. He moved his right hand down to his penis and starting stroking, thinking of Holly, fantasizing about going down on her, getting on top of her, thrusting.

"Dammit!" Jerry cursed as he flung off the covers and laid there in his boxers. "What's fucking wrong with me?" he called up to the ceiling.

He closed his eyes, and as if from out of nowhere, sleep came over him, and this time, Jerry didn't awaken until his cell phone started ringing. He checked the small digital window on the cheap alarm clock on the night table next to the bed. It read 8:02.

He reached over and got his phone on the night table next to the clock. He looked at the screen but didn't recognize the number. Finally, he pressed the answer button and mumbled, "Hello?"

"Hi, Jerry?" It was Holly.

Jerry sat up and asked, "Yeah? What's up?"

"I—I was wondering if you could come over."

"Come over?"

"Or I could come over there, see you."

"Come over for what? See me for what?"

"I really need to talk to you." She sighed. "Explain some things."

Jerry swallowed. He told himself that she was up to her actress tricks, probably for Jeff.

"Where's Jeff?"

"He's out," Holly said. "He got up early, arranged to meet a guy over on the west side, to buy a gun. The guy's a former client, or someone Jeff met in prison. I'm not sure which. Anyway, the guy supposedly can get him a stolen gun."

"For Sharkey," Jerry said.

"Yes, for Sharkey," Holly agreed. "Then, after getting the gun, he's gonna go scout him out. Follow him around. See if and when he's vulnerable, so he can sneak up and plug him in the back of the head. At least, that's how Jeff put it." She sighed. "Anyway, Jeff said he'd be gone all morning. So, I figured…I figured, it was a good time to see you, talk about things."

"Like what things, Hol?"

"About what happened to us," Holly said. "About our future."

"We have no future Holly," Jerry said. "Maybe once we did, maybe even the time I brought you down to Florida. But after that…" He laughed suddenly. "You set me up for murder, for Christ's sake."

"That was Jeff," she argued, the urgency rising in her voice. "All Jeff. I didn't know. He just showed up, and then you showed up, and he did what he did. I didn't know…"

"Look, Holly, I—"

"I'll make it worth your while," she said in a fawning voice. "For…you know."

The fantasy of just a few hours ago popped into Jerry's head. Going down on her, screwing her, with her new, phony dark hair. It'd be like screwing the evil witch out of a Disney movie, every boy's secret fantasy. He closed his eyes and tried to resist the idea, the fantasy coming true. He really tried.

"Jerry?"

"I'll be right over."

Chapter Thirty-Two
Betrayal

Jerry cursed himself the entire ride over. But he couldn't make himself turn around, call her back, tell her to go fuck herself. He told himself it would kill some time, be an interesting diversion against the shit-storm that was coming tonight. He'd play with it for a while, and then tell her, no, can't do it, can't betray Jade, can't give up what his life had become. No way. He had too much to lose—Jade, the baby. But the evil part in him, like every man had, said, *Jade'll never find out. What're you worried about?* Holly was, after all, still his wife; and, she was still damned sexy and hot. That damned evil Disney witch popped into his mind again.

Going down. Screwing her. And getting back at Jeff in a big, manly way.

At eight forty-five, Jerry knocked at the door to Holly's room, number 216. A jet taking off roared overhead. She opened the door and smiled at him.

"Hi, Jerry," she whispered as she licked her lips. She took his hand and led him inside. It was dark and musty, and the bed was unmade. For a moment, Jerry was revolted by the thought that Jeff Flaherty had slept in it the night before. That almost brought him to his senses, but in the next moment, Holly had stepped close to him and was looking up into his eyes. He could feel her breasts against him and saw the want in her eyes. He felt lost, under her control. He bent down and kissed her. Their tongues entwined. They had done it so many times before, during their marriage, but now it was different, new and exciting. It was as if she was a different woman.

Finally, Holly backed away from the kiss and whispered, "C'mon." She took his hand and pulled him onto the bed.

It was over fast, in half an hour. The going down, the screwing. Afterwards, Holly laid in his arms and, for a time, neither of them could find a thing to say.

"Why wasn't it that good when we were married?" Jerry asked.

"We are married," Holly said.

"Yes, we are," he said and smiled to himself.

They fell silent again, then Holly said, "You're a different guy. New. This has changed you."

"It's changed all of us." He rolled on his side and looked at her and Holly turned to him. "How's it with Jeff?" he asked.

She got quiet, rolled back and stared up at the ceiling. After a time, she turned to Jerry and said, "Jeff? He's an asshole. A sicko. He's gotten worse after prison. I…I can't deal with him anymore." She turned sideways and moved close to Jerry. He found himself wrapping his arms around her naked shoulders. "I don't want to be with him anymore, after this."

"So don't."

"I want to be with you."

Jerry moved away from Holly and laid his head back down on the pillow. Staring up at the ceiling, he said, "You know that can't happen. That I have someone else."

"Jade."

"Yes, Jade. And something else…a child. A son."

He felt Holly tense up next to him. He looked over and saw her forlorn, defeated look. The news seemed too much for her to bear.

"So this can never be more than this," she said. She scrunched up to him, and he put his right arm under her and brought her close. "Sex," Holly added. "Really, I never thought it would be, after what happened. After what I did. How could you trust me? I just hoped that when the time comes, you'd forgive me, and help me get away from him, Jeff." She laughed. "Use your powers as the Anonymous Man."

He almost let it go, almost told her the real deal—that the plan he had concocted with them yesterday was phony. That the real plan was to put her and Jeff back in jail and Sharkey with them. That he had no intention of sharing what was left of the Global money.

"Well, we'll see, Holly," he said. "We'll see."

She turned to him and got so close it seemed she hoped to jump into his skin. "Please, Jerry," she pleaded. "You have to help me. I need you. And I know you still care about me. That deep inside there, you…you love me."

Jerry closed his eyes and again got within a moment of revealing the truth, and of putting his trust in her again. But instead, he said, "We'll see, Holly. Once Sharkey and Fox are no longer threats, we'll see." He sighed. "Look, I better go. He might come back."

"I really screwed up, didn't I, Jerry? I should have just done it. Gone to Binghamton and become your front. Had I, we'd be sitting on some beach somewhere instead of doing this."

He shrugged and said, "I don't know. Probably."

Shaking her head, she moved away from him and sat up. She didn't seem to care, or notice, that she was naked before him. That after all their time together, it didn't matter.

"Think about it, okay? Helping me, once the dust settles."

"I will," he said. "I promise." He felt bad for saying that, knowing that in the end, he'd betray her.

"But you're right though," she said. "You should get going. Last thing I need is for him to walk in on this."

Jerry felt that she was telling the truth. That this wasn't a setup. That Jeff didn't know that she'd call him, entice him to come over. That she'd want to make love with him again.

In the next moment, she turned and crawled up to him and kissed him again. He let her, but it was a short kiss, a goodbye kiss. She moved away from him, slid off the bed. Naked, she walked toward the bathroom.

"Where you going?" he called to her, thinking maybe there was time for another romp in bed.

"Take a shower," she replied. "Let yourself out, okay?" she added as she entered the bathroom and closed the door.

As she closed the bathroom door, Jerry cursed himself again for coming here, for doing what he'd done. Betraying Jade, betraying everything he had become. Giving into Holly. Again. But in the end, he'd have the last laugh.

He laid there for a time and almost fell asleep to the continuous sound of water splashing across Holly's body from the bathroom shower. Finally, he forced himself to get up and sat for a moment, yawning on the edge of the bed. Finally, he pushed himself off and dressed. He was heading toward the door, thinking again how he'd so thoroughly and perhaps irrevocably messed up when he heard someone inserting a key card into the doorway. He stepped back and turned and somehow made it into the small closet in the corner of the room, just past the bathroom, as the person using the key opened the door.

It was Jeff, of course.

Chapter Thirty-Three
In the Closet

From the closet, Jerry heard Jeff come into the room and toss car keys onto a dresser. He called, "Hey, Lucy, I'm home. Got some 'splaining to do." He laughed to himself and seemed to have jumped onto the bed. The shower stopped, and the TV went on, blaring a sports show. Moments later, Holly came out of the bathroom.

"You're back," she said.

"Yeah, I'm back."

"Did you get it?"

"Yeah," Jeff said. "I got it. Two hundred bucks. The last of our fucking money. But pretty soon, that won't matter. We'll have a million bucks in the bank, and all of them—Sharkey, Fox and Jerry boy, will be dead."

"Hey, don't point that thing at me. What kind is it?"

"A Glock. It'll do the trick just fine."

"Stolen."

"Yes, of course, stolen."

"Did you follow Sharkey?" Holly asked. "You're back awful soon."

"Yeah, I followed him," Jeff said. "Come here."

Jerry imagined Holly must be standing before him, dripping, near the bed.

"So, what happened?"

"Know where the prick went?" Jeff asked. "And I said get your ass over here."

They fell silent for a time. It sounded like Holly had laid down on the bed and probably had slid under one of Jeff's arms. When they still didn't say anything, Jerry knew Jeff and Holly must be kissing.

"No, first, tell me about Sharkey," Holly finally said.

"Sharkey? That prick bastard really means to kill us," Jeff said. "I followed him this morning, right after I met Pablo and got the gun, hoping I'd get lucky and be able to take him out. But someone picked him up, one of his goons, I guess. And you know where they went? To our place. They went up there, looking for us."

"To kill us?" Jade asked.

"Yeah, why else? Looks like old Jerry boy saved our lives."

"Yes, he did," Holly whispered.

"Too bad we can't repay the favor," Jeff said. "Well, fuck him anyway. Thinks he's tough shit now. Know what I want, right? After all I did for us this morning."

"Yeah," she said unenthused. "I know what you want."

"Well, don't sound so happy about it."

Here we go, déjà vu all over again, Jerry thought. Stuck in the closet, he had to listen as Holly and Jeff kissed for a time. Then, they were writhing in each other's arms, and he was forced to wait it out. It ended like all sex, with silly, orgasmic grunts and moans of release fifteen minutes after the kissing began.

Jerry didn't know what to think about Holly calling him over that morning. It didn't seem to have any relationship to Jeff. It hadn't been a ruse. Holly had simply wanted to see him, to have sex with him; and, it made Jerry wonder if she really still cared.

"Know what I could use now?" Jeff asked from out of nowhere.

"No, what?"

"A big fat breakfast," he said.

Chapter Thirty-Four
No Answer

A minute after Jeff and Holly left for breakfast, Jerry cautiously emerged from the closet, looked around a moment, and hurried out of the room, then took the elevator to the lobby of the hotel. Once behind the wheel of his car, he started sobbing.

"Stupid, stupid, stupid," he whispered to himself as he lurched forward and gently banged his head against the steering wheel. "Fucking stupid."

Finally, he took a breath and calmed himself, trying to put his stunning lack of judgment and betrayal of Jade out of his mind. There were too many issues swirling around him now. Not least of all, he feared that Jade wouldn't listen to him and would fly up here sometime today.

It was almost noon by the time he got a quick breakfast and returned to the Stadium Inn. As he parked in front of Room

121 and got out of his car, the manager, a swarthy, heavy-set, humorless Muslim, who seemed to work 24/7, popped his head out of the small office at the other end of the building and called to him, "You stay another night?"

"Yes," Jerry called back. "I stay another night." *And tonight, you'll get a show to remember me by*, he thought. Cops invading his room to bust his kidnapping.

After a quick, hot shower, ostensibly to wipe Holly's odor and sweat off him, Jerry sat on the edge of the bed and took out his cell phone. He needed to call Jade, not to confess what he'd done, tell her how stupid he'd been and beg her forgiveness—something he'd unlikely ever do—but to give himself a sense of grounding. He needed to confirm that the tryst with Holly had been an aberration, a dream or something out of the Twilight Zone. One call to Jade would bring him back to reality. He'd regain his life.

He also needed to confirm that she'd listened to him and stayed down in Florida with the baby and Faith.

But for some reason, he waited. He stared at the phone in his shaking hand for a while. Finally, after a deep breath, he flipped it open. The screen was blank. No messages, no calls.

After another minute, he dialed Jade's number. It rang five times. No answer.

He frowned. Worried. Where was she? He was desperate to hear her voice. After a sigh, he tried her number a sixth time, thinking, *Pick up! Pick up!*

But like each of the other calls, this one ended in her voice mail, and he left the same message as the five other calls: "Honey, it's Jerry. Please call me as soon as you get this."

He started calling Faith but remembered that he didn't have the number of her new phone. She had ditched her last prepaid phone after being chased by Sharkey the other night and promised to buy a new one.

After leaving his sixth voice message, Jerry put down his phone on the bed next to him. Now, he was tormented not only by his state of mind but whether Jade and the baby were safe. Maybe this whole idea of taking care of Jeff and Holly had been stupid. Maybe running away would have been the better option.

Finally, Jerry closed his eyes. The weight of the last few days overcame his tension and concerns, and somehow, he fell asleep. But five minutes into a dreamless slumber, his cell phone rang. He woke up, his heart racing, and at first, couldn't find his phone. It was somewhere on the bed, under him. He dug it out by the fourth ring and flipped it open. Though he didn't recognize the number, he clicked anyway and said, "Hello, Jade?"

"No, it's Faith. Jade's not here. She's…she's on her way up to see you."

After a moment, Jerry said, "Shit. No. I told her, no."

"I told her no, too," Faith said. "But you know Jade. She wouldn't listen. She's got a flight this afternoon. She should be up there by this evening."

"What flight? What airline?"

"She wouldn't tell me. All she said was she needed to see you. That you were doing something crazy. She needed to stop you."

"Shit." Jerry took a deep breath, trying to think. What a mess this day was working out to be. "You okay with the baby."

"Yeah, I'm okay," Faith said. "I raised my sister and brother."

He knew that and told her he was sorry; that he trusted her with Seius like nobody else.

"He'll be fine, Jerry," Faith assured him. "Don't worry about him. Worry about Jade."

Jerry was seething now, angry at everything, at himself for giving into Holly and Jade for disobeying him. If she showed up at his room tonight, she could ruin everything.

"What's going on, Jerry. Are you okay?"

"Yeah, I'm fine. It's just, Jade should have stayed there."

"Jerry, I'm sorry," Faith went on, "I tried to tell her no, don't go. All she said was, 'he didn't want me last time either.' I don't know."

"Alright," Jerry interrupted. Last time, she had saved him from being murdered by Jeff in a hotel room in Kissimmee. "It'll be alright. Just take care of Seius, okay?"

"Okay, Jerry," Faith said. "I owe you guys. Don't worry about him."

Once he ended the call, Jerry wondered if he should call Fox and call it off. Meet Jade and go back with her to Florida and a life on the run. But no, her being there might not scuttle the whole thing. It could still go down, and he could tell her to leave, go back to Florida. He'd join her some time in the future. This time, as Jerry Shaw.

Chapter Thirty-Five
Final Arrangements

"Where the hell you been?" Fox asked when Jerry strolled into his hospital room at two that afternoon. "I thought you'd be here around noon."

As Jerry approached Fox's bed, he noticed that Fox looked better. He had color in his cheeks, and his voice was finally above a whisper, with only a hint of the wheeze he'd noticed the last two days. Fox raised the bed forward, and Jerry stopped beside it.

"I got held up," Jerry said, but he didn't tell him what had held him up. He was trying to forget that.

"What happened?"

"Nothing important," Jerry lied. "Here, I brought you a little present," he said as he placed the flash drive on Fox's lap. "Here's Jeff's admissions about killing Willie Robinson made during our meeting last night."

"Fantastic," Fox said. He picked up the flash drive and admired it a moment. "That gives us pretty much all we need, the last piece of the puzzle, except for busting Sharkey tonight."

"Is that all set?" Jerry asked.

"Yes, all set," Fox said. "Sharkey came to see me around nine this morning. I told him you'd be at the motel waiting for a call from me around nine for an update about what Holly and Jeff were up to. He seemed to buy it. Told me that's when he would go in; when you were on the phone. He'd use a battering ram or something to break down the door. He claimed those cheap motel room doors aren't much to break down."

"They aren't."

"Immediately after he left," Fox went on, "I called Dan Miller and told him that Sharkey would break in and grab you around that time, nine. He promised that he and a crew of SORT guys would be positioned in the parking lot by eight-thirty, ready to jump into action once they saw Sharkey and whoever break into your room."

"He's good, this Miller? I mean, competent."

"Yeah, the best. Believe me. The best."

Jerry nodded, but deep down, he was worried. He and Fox both knew a million things could go wrong.

"I still haven't provided Miller with any details other than that," Fox went on. "That Pete Sharkey would be involved in an attempted kidnapping at nine o'clock tonight. I didn't name the person he'd be kidnapping. So, Miller still doesn't know. He isn't happy about that, wondered why I was holding back. But I told him, 'why does that matter who the victim is?' He groused but decided to let it go. He'd find that out anyway once the bust goes down. I figured this way, if you want to back out, you still could do so without any repercussions. You could remain anonymous."

"Thanks for that," Jerry said. "But I've already made up my mind. Life on the run is no life. It's time for Jerry Shaw to come back from the dead."

After a shrug, Fox said, "One thing you should know. You saved Holly and Jeff's lives by getting them out of their flat last night. Sharkey and one of his goons went up there first thing this morning before he came to see me. And they didn't go for coffee."

Jerry already knew that from his detour in the closet of Holly and Jeff's hotel room. Still, he pretended not to know.

"Shit, really?"

"He was really pissed they weren't there," Fox went on. "That somehow they skipped out without being seen. One more complication still to take care of after he captures you. The guy obviously has no conscience."

"Once he's got my money, if that was what was really going down tonight, he'll kill me, too."

"Yes, I think so," Fox said. "And very likely after that, me. All the witnesses of the fake insurance scam would be gone. You and Holly and Jeff and me."

"Well, then it'll be a good thing to put him out commission."

"No doubt about that," Fox said. "Miller has some dirt on him as well. He left the U.S. Marshal's service under a black cloud, and he hasn't done much in private life to spruce up his image. The state police have had him on their radar for some time now for things like extortion, and they even suspect his involvement in a couple murders. But the guy's clever. Always seems to slip by. Like I said, his MO has been to never leave witnesses. Bringing him down will be a good thing. A service to humanity."

"When are you giving Miller the flash drive? With Jeff's admissions."

"After he busts Sharkey, he can go pick up Jeff and Holly. They're at the Holiday Inn, right?"

"Yes," Jerry said. He looked down and seemed distracted. His betrayal of Jade had crept back into his mind, as well as her taking the trip up here.

"What's the matter?" Fox asked.

With a grimace, Jerry looked down at Fox and said, "I think we may have a complication."

"What kind of complication?"

"Jade," Jerry said. "She's flying up here, to Buffalo."

"Shit, Jerry, when?"

"I have no idea," Jerry replied. "All I know is she was going to hop on a flight from Orlando this afternoon. Try and stop me or help me get through this. I'm not sure which."

"You check the flights?"

"Sure, but without an airline or a time of departure, it's like looking for a needle in a haystack. There are nine flights coming into Buffalo from Orlando this evening, most of them Southwest and Jet Blue, but a couple on Delta and United as well."

Fox sighed and asked, "Does she know where you're staying?"

"Yes, I think so. Maybe. I mean, the Stadium Inn was where I stayed for a few days after we faked my death so I could watch my fake funeral. I told her about that."

"So, she probably knows."

"Probably, yes."

Fox sighed again, turned to Jerry and said, "Well, we have

to hope she doesn't arrive at the motel before nine."

Chapter Thirty-Six
At Petey's Grave

After Jerry left Fox's room and hustled out of the hospital, he wondered again whether Fox could be trusted. He worried that he was falling into a trap—one big-time double-cross. Sharkey and a goon would break down his door to his room at nine tonight, and there'd be no Senior Investigator Miller and a crew of cops to come busting in and save the day. Fox and Sharkey would make Jade hand over the stolen Global insurance money to them.

Still, he again determined that Fox had to be trusted. It was either that or somehow find Jade on whatever flight she'd taken and drive back down to Florida to start a life on the run.

With still too many hours to kill, Jerry found himself driving around for a time. After an aimless tour of a revitalized downtown Buffalo on a gloomy, chilly Wednesday afternoon in late October, Jerry decided to take a ride out to his sister's house. Joan lived in Tonawanda, a middle-class, northern suburb of Buffalo with modest homes in quiet, safe neighborhoods. For some reason, Jerry felt the need to spend some time parked near her house and perhaps get a glimpse of Joan and Jack Reeves, her husband of many years, an accountant. And, of course, his father, Peter Shaw, Sr, nicknamed "Big Pete" because he was six-foot-two. Jerry and Joan's younger brother, Peter Shaw Jr., who everyone called Petey, had inherited his father's height and athletic build while Joan and Jerry had inherited their mother's short stature and wider girth—aka, big bones.

It had been over a year since Jerry had last seen Joan and Big Pete as they stood solemnly, praying at the family gravestone in Holy Cross Cemetery. Buried under that heavy, granite stone were his mother, dead now fourteen years, and Petey. Petey had died seventeen years ago in a tragic car crash on his way home from a party after his last Friday night high school football game his senior year. He had already signed a letter of intent to play at Michigan State the following season on a full scholarship, with the promise of a career in the NFL looming after that. That prospect had also fueled the dreams of Pete and Mary Shaw. But all those high hopes and dreams had come crashing down when Petey had foolishly taken a ride from a distant friend who'd had a little too much to drink at the party and decided to go speeding down a rain-slick, narrow county highway on a pitch-black night. On the way, the car careened off the road and hit a tree. Petey had died instantly. The other kid had walked away with only bruises.

It was around three by the time Jerry pulled along the curb in front of 67 Arbor Lane on the quiet, tree-lined street a few houses down and on the other side of Joan's quaint, three-bedroom, nicely kept Cape Cod house at 89 Arbor Lane. A month ago, while perusing the real estate transactions section of the online *Buffalo News*, as was his habit, Jerry had noted that Big Pete had sold the family home on Norfred Avenue in Lackawanna for $110,000. The sale could only mean that Big Pete had finally agreed to move out of the stale old house and move in with Joan. Joan and Jack certainly had enough room. They'd never had kids, the reason for which had never been made clear to Jerry, whether it was by choice or due to some medical issue. Seeing Big Pete's now thirteen-year-old Buick Century parked on one side of the short driveway leading to an attached two-car garage confirmed that the old man was staying there.

Jerry sat there for a time, thinking back to the weeks and months following the death of Petey. It still bothered him that his brother's death had squeezed all desire and happiness out his mother and drove her to an early grave. For the most part, it seemed, his father had lost all hope as well, especially after his mother died. He was a silent, glum man to begin with, and his distance only increased after that. Joan had once confided to Jerry that this bothered her as well. It was as if she and Jerry didn't matter, and their parents would have been content to have only raised Petey. But Joan had urged Jerry not to judge their parents too harshly. After all, losing a child was the worst possible thing in life, especially a special, talented son like Petey.

At the time, Jerry felt that he was nothing special, that he possessed no talent that could replace Petey's shine and potential. He was overweight, frumpy, and lousy at sports. Big Pete had sometimes joked, while Petey was still alive, that Jerry must have been the fat old mailman's son. Still, it bothered him to this day that his parents seemed to have developed no real connection with him, or Joan, for that matter, other than through the link of familial genetics. He wished that they could see him now. After all, he had become a kind of real-life superhero.

Sitting there watching the house at 89 Arbor Lane had awakened these old wounds and sour grievances. He sighed and closed his eyes for a time, wishing he hadn't come. The last few days had exhausted him, and as he sat there, Jerry had to pull himself from the edge of sleep. As he opened his eyes, he saw the late model Chevy Malibu, that had been parked next to his father's Buick Century, backing out of the driveway. Joan was driving, and Big Pete was in the passenger seat. As they drove off down Arbor Lane, Jerry followed after them.

Twenty-minutes later, they pulled into Holy Cross Cemetery, and Jerry drove in after them. Of course, he knew they were going to the Shaw family grave.

They slowly drove down the narrow roads that crisscrossed the many sections of the expansive cemetery, where thousands had been buried since the early 1800s. Finally, they came to a wide section with a bronze plaque on a green pole designating it as "Angels of Heaven." Directly across from it lay a long, community mausoleum where dozens of bodies were entombed above-ground.

Holly had requested that the urn containing Jerry's fake ashes be deposited at the far-right plot of the four-person grave that his father purchased after Petey's tragic death. The plots now contained, in order, the remains of Jerry's mother at the far-left side, with a plot directly to the right of her awaiting Big Pete's death, followed by Petey's grave, and next, the buried urn containing Jerry's fake ashes. Holly had even opted to purchase a fifth plot to the right of Jerry's. Of course, that had been for show as she never intended to use it. Joan, and even Big Pete were touched by the gesture though undoubtedly everyone knew that a woman so young and pretty would certainly, and most likely, very quickly, land another husband.

Marking the family grave was a squat, heavy granite stone put down shortly after Petey's death with the name "Shaw," chiseled in thick, black letters across the front. In a row of carvings across the bottom were the names, Mary Shaw, Peter Shaw, Sr., Peter Shaw Jr., Jerry Shaw and Holly Shaw. For Mary Shaw, Peter Shaw, Jr., and Jerry Shaw, their dates of birth and death had also been carved on the stone, while for Big Pete and Holly, only their dates of birth.

Joan parked on a small patch of grass at the edge of the section, and moments later, Jerry parked a few car lengths behind them. As Joan and Big Pete slowly ambled across the section around various stones to the Shaw gravestone, Jerry got out of his car and leaned against it. After a moment, he walked toward the Shaw stone as well. After a time, he stopped and pretended to pray before a gravestone that gave him a clear view of Joan and Big Pete. Jerry had no fear of being recognized. First, he was quite literally dead to them, and second, he looked nothing like the frumpy, jowly, unathletic and physically unappealing Jerry Shaw they would remember. He had become the Anonymous Man.

For a couple long minutes or so, Joan and Big Pete stood next to each other staring down at the Shaw stone. An urge struck Jerry to walk over there and reveal himself, tell them everything. Out of nowhere, Big Pete started sobbing. Joan stepped his way, and he leaned into her.

"It's okay, Dad," she said to him.

"Petey," he moaned. "My Petey." With Joan still holding onto him, he lurched into tears and bent forward as if he were about to throw up.

Twenty-yards away, Jerry scowled as he watched his father still grieving for his younger brother. Finally, the old man stood up and took a breath. He turned to Joan and said, "Let's go."

Jerry turned and walked back to his car. He slammed the door after getting in, and Joan and Big Pete glanced his way. He stared back at them. There wasn't a hint of recognition in either of them. Finally, Jerry turned the key and drove off.

Chapter Thirty-Seven
320 Northview Lane

As Jerry made a left turn out of Holy Cross Cemetery onto South Park Avenue, he decided to continue his nostalgia tour to kill more time until nine o'clock. First on the list was the house he and Holly had lived in for almost seven years at 320 Northview Lane.

To get there, Jerry continued south on South Park, passing Marzulak's Funeral Home, where his fake viewing had been held for two days before his fake funeral mass at the Our Lady of Victory Basilica, a quarter mile north up the other way, followed by his fake burial at Holy Cross Cemetery. He drove on for about five miles after that until turning right onto Big Tree Road. After a quarter mile or so, he turned left onto Northview Lane that led into the sprawling Big Tree Subdivision. Six houses on the left side of Northview, and there it was, his former residence, a three-bedroom Colonial with an attached garage. It was in that garage where Jeff had set the fire that burned the cadaver from the University of Buffalo Medical School given to them by Willie Robinson for two thousand bucks. The resulting explosion and red-hot fire had reduced the hapless cadaver to a pile of ash and mud under an old Sunbird with a gas leak that Jerry had supposedly been trying to fix.

"Poor dumb shit," one of the volunteer firemen had mumbled while shaking his head as he looked at the mess of what formerly was a human body on the wet floor of the garage under the Sunbird. He and his colleagues had put out the blaze called in by a neighbor who happened to be walking past the house just after eight that morning. The arson investigators gave this remark some credence when they concluded that a spark arcing from an old water heater into the pool of gasoline under the Sunbird had likely caused the explosion and resultant fire. The fake Jerry had thus been both unlucky and stupid— not only for buying an old car with a gas leak, but also for crawling underneath the old car next to a pool of gasoline that had leaked from it, at the exact moment, supposedly, when the old water heater in the garage launched a spark of electricity that landed in the pool.

Holly had sold the house more than two years ago during her first criminal trial so she could pay her lawyer. Like his father's house, Jerry had seen the conveyance reported in the *Buffalo News*. Holly had made a decent profit from the sale and Jerry was a little miffed because half of that money belonged to him. Holly had sold the place to a man and woman with a Polish name, Pelowski or something. When he read that, he hoped the Pelowskis had three or four kids. That's what the house needed, a family, the laughter and wailing of children, something Holly and Jerry had been unable to provide. *The place is better off,* Jerry thought bitterly. *Holly and I were a sad, woeful presence.*

After a sigh and thinking back to those days, Jerry was about to start the car and drive off, when he spotted his former next-door neighbor, Gladys Kovach, a woman of about sixty, peeking out at him from the side of the curtain hanging across the living room picture window. After a moment, Jerry smiled and waved back at her, and laughed as she hastily stepped back from the window with a shocked look.

Mrs. Kovach had been called as a prosecution witness at Holly and Jeff's murder trials to identify Jeff visiting Holly on numerous occasions both before and after Jerry's fake death. Even before that, Jerry and Holly used to laugh at Mrs. Kovach's incessant prying. They even nicknamed her "Gladys Kravitz" after the nosy neighbor from the 1960's sitcom, *Bewitched.*

Better go, Jerry thought. This time, he started the car. Seeing the house again had only re-ignited his regret and sadness over the failure of his love affair with Holly that had started out with such great promise. He gave 320 Northview Lane one last look, and drove off.

Ten minutes later, he pulled into the parking lot of the Stadium Inn. It was only a quarter after four. Still, almost five hours to kill. In his room, he tried Jade's cell but there was no answer, and this time, he left no message. Perhaps she was up in the air flying right into the middle of what could be an awful mess.

Jerry played over in his mind what Fox had told him about what he should be doing in his room at nine o'clock.

Fox had said: "Be on the bed watching TV and just let them bust in. They'll probably hold a pistol on you. Just cooperate with Sharkey, and whoever is with him. Sit still, nod a lot, agree, whatever, and wait for Miller and his men to make their move. And when that happens, you hit the floor and keep your head down. Hopefully, Sharkey and his men won't be stupid enough to put up a fight or start shooting, or something. But you never know. Don't participate, don't try and help Miller. Do as I say and just lay low."

That pep talk hadn't done much for Jerry's morale. Sharkey seemed like the type of guy likely to fight back and ask questions later. How was he to know they were cops? And the last thing Jerry needed was for Jade to walk into the middle of that. He got out of bed and used his laptop to try and figure one last time what flight she was coming up on. There were four flights in the air right now. He tried her cell number again and got the same result. No answer. Was she up there, on one of them, her cell on airplane mode?

His thoughts turned again to the house at 320 Northview Lane. Suddenly, he didn't regret anything. He was glad that it had turned out to be an unhappy house and that his memories of it, overall, were distasteful. After all, because of those unhappy memories, he had ended up with Jade. He had become the Anonymous Man.

Chapter Thirty-Eight
Rochester

Despite the thoughts and worries roiling through his mind, Jerry closed his eyes and fell asleep. He woke from his nap around six, starving. Having dinner somewhere would kill even more time until zero hour.

He wanted to be back in his motel room around eight. He knew that the seconds would tick slowly to an event that would forever change his life—again—and might even kill him. But the alternative, to spend the rest of his days on the run with Jade and the baby in tow, desperate to stay one step ahead of Holly and Jeff and guys they hired like Pete Sharkey, still wasn't appealing.

He went to a Greek diner on South Park Avenue in Blasdell about a ten-minute ride from the motel. He ordered the hamburger plate and gobbled it down without pleasure. As he ate, he was still distracted by what was to go down in a couple hours.

After dinner, he called Fox.

"It's still a go," Fox said. "One hundred percent. Miller and his men will be there. Remember what I told you. How to handle things when things go down."

"Yeah," Jerry said, taking one last bite of the burger. After a swallow, he added,

"Cooperate with Sharkey, hit the floor when Miller and his guys bust in."

"Yes," Fox said. "Don't try and be a hero, or a superhero." After a sigh, he asked, "Anything from Jade?"

"No, nothing," Jerry said. "I have no idea where she is. I've been calling and calling. I don't get an answer."

"If she's flying…"

"I know."

"Well, we can call it off for tonight."

"No, let's do it. We may not get a second chance."

"Alright." Fox sighed. "Remember what I told you. Just sit there, cooperate, and then when Miller busts in, hit the floor."

"I know, I got it."

At 8:05, Jerry was back in his room. He laid on the bed and put on the TV and kept changing the channels. None of it mattered. It was just noise, flashes of images. He couldn't concentrate. After a time, he reached for his cell phone on the night table next to the bed and called Jade again.

And again, she didn't answer.

As Jade disembarked the plane, her cell phone rang. She looked down at the number. It was Jerry. *Don't answer*, she told herself.

She had taken a flight to Rochester, to avoid any chance

that Jerry would find her, stop her from helping him. But now she had an hour and a half drive to Buffalo, and the flight had been half an hour late. That meant, she wouldn't arrive at the motel where she knew he must be staying—the Stadium Inn—until nearly nine.

She made her way to one of the rental car counters on the first level of the terminal where she had booked a car, a medium-sized sedan. They gave her a navy-blue Chevy Cruze. By 7:15, she was finally driving out of the terminal lot and onto Interstate 490. There was still a good chance she'd make it to Jerry's room before nine and could talk him out of doing what he was about to do. She'd rather be on the run with the Anonymous Man than to have Jerry spend time in prison separated from her and Seius.

She also wondered if upon her arrival at his room, she'd have to rescue him again, save him from mortal danger. The problem, of course, was that this time Jade didn't have a gun.

Chapter Thirty-Nine
Miller Time

Since five that evening, Jeff and Holly had parked the rented Toyota Corolla in the lot at 7-Eleven across the street from the building where Sharkey had his office. It was now close to eight and Holly squirmed in her seat.

"How long do we have to wait here?" she asked. "I have to pee."

"I told you not to get that diet coke," Jeff hissed and glared across at her a moment.

"I was thirsty," she whined. "And now I'm hungry. Why didn't we eat first?" Holly turned to him. "Why did you bring me along anyway?"

"Because two sets of eyes are better than one," Jeff replied.

"What are we waiting around to see?" Holly asked. "Why not go up there and blast him. I don't get it."

"Yeah, like he's gonna let us do that." He laughed to

himself. "Walk up to him and blast him. There's surveillance cameras all over the place on this building looking at anything that comes into the parking lot. Including us."

"Where?"

Jeff pointed out two, both high up on silver poles that Sharkey must have had installed. He apparently had made some enemies along the way since he left the U.S. Marshal's Service, and most likely, before he retired.

"So what are we waiting for then? What's the plan?"

"For him to leave," Jeff said. "See if he makes any stops on his way home to that mansion of his in Amherst."

"You can't shoot him at his house?"

"Not likely," Jeff said. "There'll be cameras there, too. I mean, as a last resort. Hide out at the next-door neighbor's and surprise him first thing in the morning when he leaves for work. Better than that is to get him at some stop-off along the way. Tonight, if possible."

"Sounds like getting him isn't going to be easy."

"That's cause it's not going to be easy," Jeff said with some annoyance in his voice. "It's going to be quite difficult, in fact. Sharkey's a professional. A killer, probably. He's got enemies, like I said, so he's the type of guy who stays alert. We just have to catch him at the right moment, when his defenses are down, and get lucky. After all, he won't be expecting us. We still have the element of surprise. That's why we have to watch him, go slow, be methodical about it."

"Why don't we just get Jerry's money and pack up and get the hell out of here?" Holly asked.

"Because, I told you," Jeff said. "Sharkey wants that money, too. All of it. He'll screw that Fox idiot out of it, probably kill him, too. A million bucks is a lot of money, gives a guy like Sharkey a lot of incentive. There's no way he won't come after us if we double-cross him."

"We'd not be double-crossing him," Holly argued. "He's already double-crossing us."

Jeff sighed, too tired or exasperated to continue the discussion.

"Well, when does he go home?" Holly asked and whined a little more. "I told you, I have to pee."

Jeff ignored her squirming next to him for a time. He turned to her and said, "Pee into your goddamn empty coke can if you have to go that bad. That's the only thing I can tell you."

"Ew! I'm not doing that." She sighed disagreeably. "I'd rather pee in my pants." She looked back toward the building behind them. "How can a 7-Eleven not have a bathroom?"

Suddenly, Jeff said, "Shut up. There he is, coming out."

They watched as Pete Sharkey hurried from the entrance of the building across the street to a late model black Ford Focus next to silver Lexus SUV. He got in and backed out of the parking space.

"There he goes," Jeff said and glanced at Holly as he started the Corolla. "But that's not his car. Must be a rental. Now, you'll just have to hold it, or go in your pants."

"He's alone," Holly commented. "None of his goons are with him."

"Yep," Jeff agreed. "All by his lonesome. Bad for him, good for us."

"Why's he driving a rental instead of his Lexus? A Ford Focus no less?"

"I have no idea," Jeff said.

The Focus took a left turn out of the parking lot, and after waiting a few seconds, Jeff started out after it. Sharkey turned right onto Walden Avenue. After a ten-minute drive, he entered the Thruway westbound just past the Galleria Mall. This, too, was strange. He was going the opposite way from his home.

"Where the hell's he going?" Jeff mumbled to himself.

They followed him on the Thruway past the entrance to the I-190, the interstate that headed into downtown Buffalo, and remained a few car lengths behind as Sharkey pulled onto the ramp for the Route 219 expressway that led to the rural southtowns like Colden and Springville and Ellicottville. But Sharkey wasn't going all the way down there. After only a couple miles on the expressway, he took the exit onto Milestrip Road, and after another couple of miles on Milestrip, the Focus turned left onto Abbott Road. After passing New Era Cap Stadium, where the Buffalo Bills played, Sharkey made a right onto Southwestern Boulevard. Not long after that, Jeff slowed when he saw the Focus' right turn blinker.

"Holy shit," Jeff said as he sped past where the Focus had just turned. "He's pulled into the Stadium Inn. Where Jerry's staying."

Jeff drove past the Stadium Inn for a time until he found a left turn lane, turned around and headed back toward the motel. On the way back, Holly spotted a RaceTrac gas station and demanded that Jeff stop a minute and let her finally relieve herself. With a groan, he agreed. After five minutes, she was back in the car, and they were driving back toward the Stadium Inn. It was eight-fifteen and completely dark when Jeff turned left into the motel parking lot. Heavy clouds loomed low in the sky on a chilly late October night.

Jeff drove the length of the lot, craning his neck, trying to find where Sharkey had parked. "Where'd he go?" He pulled into a spot across from the two-story, L-shaped motel with fifty rooms. He kept the car idling as he looked at the quiet lot. All the cars were parked. Nobody came out of the five or six occupied rooms, and no other cars drove in.

"That's gotta be it," Jeff said, nodding toward a room. "Jerry's room."

"Which one?"

"Room 121. The one with the Rogue in front of it. Jerry was driving a Rogue, remember?"

"I don't know cars," Holly replied.

With the car still idling, Jeff shrugged and continued looking for Sharkey.

"Where the fuck is he?" he wondered. "And why's he come here tonight? I thought the thing with Jerry was going down tomorrow night." He looked at Holly. "That's what Jerry-boy told us."

"I have no idea," Holly said.

In the next moment, a caravan of three cars pulled into the lot one after the other. Jeff turned off his car and hissed, "Get down." He reached out his hand and pulled Holly down to him. Jeff stayed just up enough so that he could see through the steering wheel over the console.

"What's happening?" Holly whispered after a time.

"Yeah, that was him," Jeff said. "In one of the cars. I'm sure of it."

"Who?" Holly asked. "Who was him? Who'd you see?"

"Miller, that's who, the investigator from the state police," Jeff said. "The prick who helped Jack Fox put us in jail."

Chapter Forty
An Unexpected Visitor

At 8:35, three unmarked police sedans, black Dodge Chargers, on loan from the state police's Special Operations Response Team, pulled into the parking lot of the Stadium Inn. Two of them took spots along the main building, one near the office and the other at the far end, while the car in which Senior Investigator Dan Miller rode parked in the second row only a few spots away from Jeff and Holly's rental. Each sedan had two occupants: a driver and a passenger. They wore their SORT gear—black shirts and pants, bulletproof vests and head mikes. It was something out of a Navy SEALs team raid and, in fact, SORT members liked to believe that the SEALs had nothing on them.

After scanning the lot and the motel, and seeing no activity, Miller spoke into his mike to the SORT team members put together especially for this operation. "Okay, boys," he said, "settle in. ETA is nine." He checked his watch. "Twenty minutes, then we engage."

Across from Miller's car, Jeff stuck his head up again and asked, "What the fuck is going on? They gonna raid Jerry?"

"Maybe Fox turned him in," Holly suggested.

"Fox is working with Sharkey, remember?"

Holly shrugged and asked, "So, what's happening?"

"Right now, nothing," Jeff said. "They're just sitting there, watching things, waiting for something."

"What?"

"Fuck if I know."

"Should we do anything?" Holly asked.

"Like what?"

"Call Jerry?"

Jeff nodded after a moment, lowered his head, and scrunched down into his seat. He pulled out his cell phone out and dialed the number Jerry had given him. It rang four times, then went to voicemail, where a metal woman's voice asked the caller to leave a message.

"Fuck it," Jeff said. He ended the call and said, "He didn't pick up."

At almost the same moment, from inside Room 121, Jerry looked at the number on the screen of his cell phone and wondered why Jeff was calling.

Senior Investigator Miller pulled out his cell phone and called Fox.

"Yeah?"

"Jack, we're in place."

"Good. Anything happening?"

"Not yet."

"Later on, the lot will fill up," Fox suggested. "Be packed by Midnight."

"I had one of my guys alert the manager," Miller said.

"Alright, good," Fox said. "As soon as Sharkey goes in, you pounce."

"Roger that. We'll be in there before he can think what to do."

"He'll be armed," Fox said. "And you already know, he's dangerous. Also, he might have one or two of his goons with him."

"I've briefed the team on what a dangerous scumbag Sharkey is."

"Okay, good," Fox said. "Keep me posted."

"Copy that."

Five minutes later, at ten to nine, Miller called him back.

"The occupant of Room 121 just got a visitor," Miller told Fox. "Some woman."

"Shit," Fox said.

"That change anything?"

Fox thought a moment. "No. Negative. Carry on."

"Roger that," Miller said. "You know who she is?"

"No," Fox lied. In fact, he did.

It was Jade.

Chapter Forty-One
Nine

"What the fuck's she doing here?" Jeff asked no one in particular.

"Who?"

"That whore of his," Jeff said. "She just walked into his room."

"Jade?"

"Yeah, fucking Jade."

Holly shook her head. "I have no idea."

Jerry had been kissing Jade when his cell rang with an annoying jingle. Jerry saw that it was Fox and he picked up right away. As he did so, Jade backed away and sat down on the bed.

"Jesus, Jerry," Fox said and sighed. "This complicates things, big time, her being there."

"What can I say?" Jerry said and looked at Jade with a smile.

"She's persistent, resourceful."

"Do you want to call it off?" Fox asked. "We've got ten minutes."

Still looking down at Jade, he said, "No, it's decided. We're gonna end the charade once and for all. Take our lumps. Start living like real people again. Living people. Not ghosts."

"Alright," Fox said. "It's your call. But I'll call Sharkey and tell him you told me Jade's there. This way, they'll be no surprises. And you still need to do what I told you."

"Yeah, I know," Jerry said. "Cooperate. Lay low. Hit the floor when the shit hits the fan. I told Jade, and she understands."

After a sigh, Fox said, "Alright, let's do this."

A minute later, Fox called back and said, "Alright, Sharkey's been alerted."

"What did he say?"

"He said, fine, better yet, makes getting the money easier," Fox told Jerry. He sighed and added, "One last time. Abort or go?"

"Let's do it," Jerry and nodded at Jade next to him on the bed as he reached out and held her hand. "Go."

"Alright, be safe my friend," Fox said and hung up.

The cheap alarm clock on the night table told Jerry it was 8:57.

At three minutes to nine, Miller checked in with his two units.

"Three minutes," he told them. A minute passed. "Two minutes."

Miller knew Sharkey would be good about the time. He was programmed from his training and all his years of experience, to execute a bust or a raid on time, to the second. Kidnapping Jerry had been scheduled for nine o'clock, and Miller felt confident that at nine o'clock it would go down.

Still, he was bothered by something. The parking lot and the motel were too quiet, and there was no sign that Sharkey and any of his goons were there. Miller had scanned the cars in the parking lot around him with his binoculars, and though the occupants could be laying low in their respective cars, below his line of sight, he found that unlikely. Why would they hide?

Miller checked his watch again. 8:59. The seconds ticked by. He waited, looked up, then down again, and his watch still read 8:59.

"Jesus," he hissed to himself.

Finally, it clicked forward.

To nine.

Chapter Forty-Two
Found Again

At five after nine, Miller called Fox and said, "Nothing's happening. Nothing."

Fox didn't know what to say. Sharkey had assured him that he was going to burst into Jerry's room at nine o'clock sharp, nab him, and wrest control of the million dollars. Easy pickings, especially now with Jade there.

"Give it another few," Fox said. "I don't know what to tell you. I haven't heard anything."

"Alright," Miller said, with some annoyance in his voice. If this didn't go down, if this was a false alarm, he'd have wasted a lot of assets and a whole lot of overtime pay. And the SORT commander from whom he'd beg to loan him a crew of five of his men would be pissed.

At a quarter after nine, Miller called Fox back and said, "Still nothing, Jack." He sighed. "Pretty soon, I'll have to call off the dogs. These guys need to get home. They were on a drug raid last night, didn't report off until four a.m. I had to beg their commander to let me use them. That I was finally bagging Pete Sharkey. Now, it's one hot mess."

"I'm sorry, Dan. What can I tell you? It was all set up. You gotta believe me."

"I believe you. But something must have changed. That girl walking in?"

"No, I called Sharkey, told him. He said fine."

"Who the hell was she? Do you know?"

"If I told you that," Fox said. "I'd give up my snitch."

"You know who she looked like?'

Fox frowned, knowing full well what Miller was going to tell him.

"Holly Shaw," Miller said. "Except she's gone back to being a blonde."

"No," Fox said. "It wasn't her."

"Who is it?" Miller asked. "The bait. Can you at least tell me that, now that it looks like a false alarm?"

"No," Fox replied. "I can't." He sighed. "I just can't. Not yet. Soon enough, believe me, you'll know."

Miller gritted his teeth, growing miffed at Fox. It had seemed odd from the very beginning that he couldn't reveal who Sharkey wanted to grab or why. But he knew from the Jeff Flaherty and Holly Shaw case that Jack Fox was a stand-up guy. His reputation with the Philly PD was impeccable, and Global had nothing but good things to say about him as well.

"Alright," Miller said, deciding to respect Fox and not press for answers right now. "Call your bait inside, whoever it is, and get back to me."

They hung up, and Fox immediately called Jerry.

"Yeah," Jerry said with an anxious sigh. "What's going on Mister Fox?"

"I have no idea," Fox said. "If Sharkey got spooked, you have any idea why? Something that happened earlier today?'

"Nothing happened," Jerry said. He tried to think back to what he'd done that day. Yes, he'd seen Holly, and there was his terrible lapse of judgment with her. He'd gone on his nostalgia tour, stopping by Joan's house and following her and his father to the Shaw family grave, followed by his look at 320 Northview Lane. All that was left of his day was a tasteless dinner and the long hours of worry and waiting that apparently had been for nothing.

"Nothing," Jerry reiterated.

"I just don't get it, then," Fox said. "You're a sitting duck in there. He knows you got the million somewhere. So, why not pounce?"

"Like I said, I have no idea, Mister Fox. None."

"What's going on?" Holly whispered.

"Nothing," Jeff hissed. "Absolutely nothing. Miller and his guys are just waiting."

"What time is it?"

Jeff checked his watch and said, "Almost nine-thirty-five." He let out a breath. "Wait a minute. There he goes."

"Who?"

"That Miller," Jeff said. "He's taking off, driving out of the lot. And the other two cars are right behind him."

"So that's it?"

Jeff sat up. "That's it."

At that exact moment, Jerry's cell phone rang. It was Fox.

"Miller called off the operation," Fox said. "He and his guys left." Jerry sighed at the news of that as Fox said, "I would get out of there. Now. Get a room at another motel. I'm frankly not sure what happened, but I don't like it one bit. With him not showing up, I smell a double-cross."

"Who's doing the double-crossing?"

"Him, Sharkey," Fox said. "He's double-crossing me. Us." Fox sighed. "Why, you think maybe I'm in on it? Double-crossing you?"

Jerry thought a moment, seeing Fox sitting there in his hospital bed. With that image in his head, Jerry decided against him being a participant in a double-cross. And anyway, he had to trust him.

"Alright, Mister Fox. I'll call you when I get to another place."

After Jerry hung up the phone, he looked at Jade sitting next to him on the bed and said, "We gotta go. Get a different motel."

"Where?"

"Anywhere," Jerry said.

"You think Fox is setting you up?" Jade asked.

"I have no clue."

In the next moment, the door leading to the room next door burst open. With tense expressions, Jerry and Jade turned to it just as Pete Sharkey strode into their room. Stalking in right behind Sharkey was Chuck Bruno. They were both carrying thick, silver pistols. *A three-fifty-seven*, Jerry thought.

Sharkey stopped at the foot of the bed and smiled down at Jerry and Jade.

"The Anonymous Man, I presume," he said. He turned to Jade and still smiling, added, "And his front."

Part Three
Lost Again

Chapter Forty-Three
Classic Fake Quadruple-Cross

"First, thing," Sharkey said, "hand over your goddamn cell phones." When Jerry and Jade hesitated, he snapped, "Now!" Noticing Jerry tense and assess the situation, with him thinking perhaps about jumping up and pouncing on them somehow, Sharkey smiled and added, "I wouldn't, Jerry." He raised the .357 and pointed it at him. "I'm a good shot."

"Put it down," Jerry said. He pulled out his cell phone and tossed it toward Sharkey at the foot of the bed. He gave Jade a nod, and a moment later she did likewise. Sharkey moved both phones close to him.

"You thought that little trick with the police would work?"

"You're all in on this?" Jerry asked as he nodded to Bruno. "You and him and Fox?"

With a laugh from the corner of the room, Chuck Bruno answered, "No, not Jack. He's too fucking straight." He added,

"You know, it was me who knocked the shit out of him down in Binghamton."

"Then, how did you know about…?"

"Ever hear of a Q-Bug, Jerry?" Sharkey asked. "My friend over here, Mister Bruno, planted one in Fox's hospital room."

"Stuck one, smaller than a postage stamp," Bruno chimed in, "on the curtain in his room. It's a voice transmitter. Has a sim card in it. All I need to do is call in, and listen, hear everything that Jack and whoever happens to be there have to say." With a grin, he went on, The wonder of modern technology. I planted it a couple days ago. Same day you walked in to visit him as his nephew. Steven, wasn't it?"

"Point is," Sharkey interrupted, "allowed us to eavesdrop on every sneaky little word you and Fox said, from day one to just a couple of minutes ago." He smirked and added, "Your classic fake double-double cross or whatever just got trumped by the classic fake quadruple-cross. Doesn't matter. What we want now is your cooperation."

"You mean, you want my money," Jerry said.

"Your money?" Bruno said with a laugh. "You mean Global Insurance's money. Money that you stole."

"And money that you're now stealing."

"Who cares? You gonna call, a cop?" Bruno laughed.

"So, where is it?" Sharkey asked and waited for Jerry to turn to him. "The money."

Jerry gave a mild shrug and looked at Jade.

"Look," Sharkey said as he picked up the phone. "We can do this the easy way, or we can do it the hard way. Torture your lady friend here, mother of your child—a son, right?—or find that bitch you've been sheltering down in Florida who's now taking care of the little lad."

Jerry tensed again, grit his teeth. He wanted to pounce. He wanted to wipe that smirk off Sharkey's face, and Bruno's after that. But he was powerless. Their pistols made him helpless.

"All you need to do is transfer the money," Sharkey went on, "from whatever account or accounts the money is in, to the one I give you. One million of it, anyway. You can keep the rest. Consider it a gesture of goodwill on our part."

"Bullshit," Jerry said. "Once I make the transfer, we're dead."

"You're already dead, Mister Shaw" Bruno said and laughed. "What difference would it make?"

"And all the more reason not to kill you," Sharkey assured Jerry and glanced over at Bruno with a scowl. "What would be gained, except more blood? Like we said, you can't exactly call the police."

With Jerry sitting there trying to assess the situation, Sharkey added, "Look, I have no time to debate this. You'll just have to take your chances. Either make the transfer right this minute, or I take both of you out to a little cabin at my disposal deep in the woods and make you do it anyway. The hard way." He glanced over at Bruno. "That's all he's been talking about since your little lady showed up here this evening, hoping that he'd get a chance to fuck her brains out to convince you to hand over the money."

Jerry seemed suddenly out of breath. He couldn't think. His heart raced. If there was a way out of this, he couldn't think of it.

"So what's it gonna be?" Sharkey asked. "The easy way, or the hard way?"

Chapter Forty-Four
The Key

As Jeff opened the driver's side door, Holly asked, "Where you going?"

"Stay here," he hissed as he slid out of the car. He nodded toward Jerry's room. "I'm going to check things out. I think it's time to use this to get our money." Jeff held up the Glock he'd bought that morning. He had loaded it in the hotel room in front of Holly before they drove out to Sharkey's office. "With his whore with him in there, we have a bargaining chip."

Jeff gently closed the door and crept toward the motel trying not to make a sound. The parking lot and motel were dark and quiet, deserted it seemed. It was still too early for horny guys to come along and get themselves and their escorts or mistresses a room. By midnight, the lot would be packed, and just about every room would be taken.

Jeff trotted the last ten yards and leaned against the far

corner of Room 122, right next to the one Jerry and Jade were in. After a few moments, Holly saw him take a breath, and finally move left, toward Jerry's room. He stopped after a moment and peeked inside the room through a small crack between the curtains of its long, greasy window. He jerked back and stood sharp and tense against the wall. Several seconds later, Jeff pushed himself away, scurried back to the rental car, and got in.

"What's the matter?" Holly asked. "I thought…"

"Shut up," Jeff snapped. "Fucking Sharkey's in there holding a gun on Jerry-boy and his whore. There's another guy with Sharkey. Has a gun, too. A bald guy. One of Sharkey's goons." He thought a moment, and added, "Bet they got in through Room 120, through the door between the rooms. When Miller and his men left, they ambushed Jerry."

After a time, Holly asked, "So now what?"

"The office," Jeff said and gestured with his head toward it at the other end of the lower floor of the main building. "Get the key to Room 120. Sneak in and do what Sharkey and the other guy did. Pop out of the door between the rooms with guns blasting. We get to kill two birds with one stone, literally. I kill Sharkey, and his goon, and we make Jerry give us the money."

"And then do what with Jerry and that whore?"

"What do you want me to do?" Jeff asked.

Holly looked away and shrugged. Finally, she turned to him and said, "Jeff, you're making this sound too easy."

After a moment, he shrugged and asked, "Maybe we're just lucky. Like getting sprung out of prison."

"I mean, too easy. Like it's easier than it seems."

"Well, you got a better idea?" He looked toward Room 121.

"It's either do that or let Sharkey get the money and come after us with his bald-headed goon. The last thing Sharkey is expecting is us. And he's preoccupied right now trying to get the money out of Jerry." As his expression hardened, Jeff said, "No, I think it can work. Let's go."

Before Holly could argue the point, Jeff was out of the car. After tucking the pistol into the waistband in the front of his jeans, and covering it with his T-shirt, he made a diagonal beeline to the motel office with Holly following a few steps behind him.

The owner of the motel, a Muslim by the look of him, was sitting on a stool behind a counter watching a repeat of *Seinfeld* on a small TV set on a cart at the far corner of the narrow office. As Jeff entered, followed by Holly, the manager stood.

"Yes? Can I help you? Need a room?"

"No, I don't need a room," Jeff said. "I need the key to Room 120."

"Sorry, that room is occupied," the owner said with a tight smile.

Jeff pulled out the pistol and pointed it at the owner.

"Fuck it," Jeff said. "Get me the fucking key, towel head. Room 120."

Holly leaned against the door jam, but tensed up when she saw Jeff's aggressive thrust of the pistol toward the owner.

"Yes, yes," the owner stuttered. "I-I get it. Room 120." He fumbled below the counter for a moment. Finally, his hand came up holding a small black snub-nose revolver.

When Jeff saw it, he moved to his left just as the owner pulled the trigger. A bullet careened off the wall behind Jeff, missing Holly by a foot. Jeff pulled the trigger of his pistol. The recoil wasn't bad, and the shot wasn't as loud as he expected. Probably couldn't be heard much outside the office. Certainly, not all the way down to Room 121, where Sharkey and his goon were holding Jerry and Jade hostage.

Jeff's shot didn't miss. It hit the owner in his upper left chest. He fell forward onto the counter and started ripping at his shirt, then jerked backward and fell to the floor in the cramped space behind the counter and the wall.

Jeff hurried behind the counter. Straddling the body of the Muslim owner, he became mildly frantic as he scanned for the room keys. "Where's the fucking keys?" he asked no one in particular.

Finally, Jeff noticed a large cabinet at the lower right side of the counter and pulled open the door. Inside, he found a series of numbered boxes corresponding to the fifty-four rooms of the motel.

"Fuck," Jeff said out of relief instead of despair. He quickly found the key to Room 120 on a blue plastic key marker. In the next moment, he got up, and after stepping over the body of the owner, he hurried out from behind the counter. Holly stood there as he moved toward her to the door.

"Let's fucking go," he barked as he moved past her.

She nodded and followed him out the door into the chilly night.

Chapter Forty-Five
Shoot-Out

Crouching, Jeff hugged the wall of the motel as he edged toward Room 120 with Holly lagging a few feet behind him, her heart beating hard, out of breath. Jeff held the pistol that he'd just fired, killing the motel owner, in his right hand pointed above his head.

Finally, Jeff made it to the door to Room 120 and stopped. He turned the knob and felt that it was locked. He took the key out of the pocket of his jeans, slowly inserted it into the lock and turned it gently to the right. He tried the knob again, and this time it turned. After pushing the door open a crack, he turned back to Holly, nodded and mimed, *Stay here.*

She nodded in return, and closing her eyes, backed up against the window of the room.

Jeff took a deep breath and pushed the door open just enough so that he could squeeze through. The room was lit by a dull, yellow glow from the lamp on the night table next to the far side of the bed. Jeff froze for a time after entering the room. The connecting door between Room 120 and Room 121 was open, and he could hear Pete Sharkey's hard-edged voice barking something at Jerry and Jade. Jeff figured the two of them must be on the bed listening wide-eyed to the blustery, over-confident Sharkey. *Boy*, Jeff thought to himself, and almost laughed, *that prima donna and his goon in the room with him are going to be in for a big surprise—their last.*

What a gift he'd been given. Instead of Sharkey and his goon, Jerry and Jade would be listening to *his* ultimatum. But not here—he'd take them back to the flat in Lackawanna where he'd strong-arm Jerry into handing over the rest of Global's money. And after that, he'd take them out to the woods somewhere and shoot them both.

Outside the room, Holly pressed her back against the window, focusing, trying to hear what Jeff was up to, knowing that he meant to kill two people, and most likely kill Jerry and Jade after that. Her heart was still beating fast, and she was having trouble breathing.

Holly couldn't get out of her mind the image of the sudden bloody wound to the Muslim motel owner's upper chest as the shot from Jeff's pistol ripped through it, followed by the man's shocked, pained expression as he crumpled forward onto the counter and fell with a jerk to the floor behind it. Jeff had grunted to himself as if pleased with this outcome.

When he'd mumbled, "Fucking Arab towel head," Holly wondered, again, what kind of man she had attached her line to. How had she not recognized from the first, during her firm's Christmas party five years ago, that Jeff was a bad guy? How had she continued screwing up all these years by staying with a man who had expressed no remorse over killing Willie Robinson, and had so easily planned to kill Jerry? And now, he seemed to have no regret after killing a totally innocent man. Of course, he would argue that he was only defending himself from the owner's attempt to shoot him, but that didn't explain why he had been gleeful after killing him. And soon, she might be called upon to help him dispose of Jerry and Jade.

Holly couldn't stand there wondering what was going on inside Rooms 120 and 121 anymore. She moved to her right and stepped into the room through the door opened only a crack, careful to keep quiet. She immediately spotted Jeff inching toward the open door between the two rooms.

Within a foot of the door, Jeff listened as Sharkey shouted, "Now give me those fucking numbers!" From his voice, Jeff determined that Sharkey was standing at the foot of the bed. But he had no idea where the bald goon was and wished he'd say something so he could get a bead on his position. Finally, he got his wish.

"Let me fuck her," the goon said.

Perfect, Jeff thought, and guessed that he must be standing along the right side of the bed. He'd be first, and Sharkey an instant later.

Now was the time. Now or never. They were oblivious to him.

After a breath, Jeff made his move. Lifting the pistol, he stepped into the open doorway between the two rooms. As expected, the bald goon was standing with a smirk on his face at the side of the bed. Jeff brought up the pistol to chest level, aimed a moment, and fired. The shot hit the side of the goon's head, leaving an instantaneous red splotch in his bald temple.

He lurched sideways, hovered a moment, and fell. Dead.

In the next instant, Jeff swiveled around toward Sharkey. For his part, Sharkey had already turned slightly to see his comrade go down. By then, Jeff had aimed his pistol at Sharkey's midsection. At the last minute, owing to his years of training and experience as a U.S. Marshal, Sharkey tilted and turned to the left just as Jeff pulled the trigger. His shot missed Sharkey's chest by an inch. This gave Sharkey time to raise his .357 and fire. This shot didn't miss. It struck Jeff square in the nose, opening a gaping, horrific wound. His entire face was suddenly a bloody pulp. He was no longer recognizable as a human being, and death was instant.

Holly tensed and went wide-eyed as she watched Jeff crumple and fall onto the musty, tan carpet in Room 120. As he fell, his arms splayed out and the pistol he'd been holding flung out of his right hand. It landed at Holly's feet, and she instinctively bent down and picked it up. She looked at the pistol in her hand, then crouched and pointed it at the open door between the rooms, her finger on the trigger. In the instant after Jeff had fallen, she had formed a plan. There was no choice but to shoot Sharkey. Or at least, try.

Sharkey loomed in the doorway. With a smirk, he looked down at Jeff for a moment, before looking up with a surprised expression to see Holly crouched there, glaring up at him. It took a moment for him to realize that she had a pistol in her hand.

"Hey, what the—"

Holly didn't let him finish. She pulled the trigger, felt the surprisingly mild recoil. The shot missed. But as Sharkey raised his .357, she pointed the pistol again and pulled the trigger. This time the shot struck Sharkey square in the forehead. He jerked backward into the door jam, tumbled sideways, and lingered momentarily as if balanced there before finally falling to the ugly carpet of Room 121. Like Jeff only moments before, Pete Sharkey had been shot dead.

Chapter Forty-Six
Escape

Jerry slid off the bed crept to the open door between the rooms a moment later. He had to step over Pete Sharkey's body on his way to the doorframe so he could peek into Room 120. The first thing he noticed was Jeff's lifeless body sprawled out unnaturally just on the other side of it. He turned and saw Holly. She was on her knees with a shocked expression, still holding the pistol in her right hand. She looked up at Jerry after a moment and slowly stood up. After a breath, she slowly walked toward him. As Holly approached Jerry, still in the doorway between the two rooms, she held out the Glock and placed it into his right hand. She proceeded to enter Room 120 and, with a blank expression, sat at the foot of the bed.

Jerry looked back at Jade, who had skirted to the edge of the bed on the other side from where Chuck Bruno's body lay. Jerry turned, and with the pistol in his hand, walked back into the room.

"Are you alright?" he asked Holly.

She nodded emptily and looked up at him. "I—I think so," she said. With a nod to Sharkey's body, she asked, "Is he dead?"

"Yes," Jerry said. "They're all dead." He looked up at Jade and nodded, almost smiled, and turned back to Holly. "You—you saved us."

Holly looked up at him and shrugged.

"Now," Jerry went on, again looking at Jade, "we need to go."

Jerry told Jade and Holly that they'd spend the night in the room Jerry had booked for Jeff and Holly at the Holiday Inn. Holly would drive over with him in the rental, and Jade would take the Rogue. Jade gave him a look, wondering why he wanted to be alone with Holly on the ride over but said nothing.

"First, we have to wipe the place down," he added. "Remove our fingerprints. And quickly."

Jade and Holly nodded, and within moments, they were using Kleenex from the two bathrooms to wipe all evidence of their being in the room, wiping down the end tables, the TV remote, and the knobs to all the doors. Finally, Jerry went to the next room and, using another Kleenex, fished the car keys out of the front pocket of Jeff's jeans. He gave a quick glance to the mess that used to be Jeff's face and shook his head. He didn't feel sorry. Jeff was a heartless killer who'd finally gotten his justice. His death had freed Jerry from having to testify about the recording in which Jeff had admitted killing Willie Robinson. As Jerry stood over Jeff's body with the keys in his right hand, he realized that, somehow, he was free again, Free to resume life as the Anonymous Man, provided he and Jade and Holly could sneak out of the motel.

From the open door to Room 121, Jerry peeked out and scanned the outside. Having heard the bangs and pops like gunfire coming from the vicinity of Rooms 120 and 121, several motel guests were milling around outside. Fortunately, they were from rooms on the other side of the motel, or upstairs.

Jerry decided that there was nothing they could do about that. They had to run for it. The motel guests would tell the cops that they saw a man and two women leaving from around the rooms where the killings had been and that they drove off in separate cars. What it had to do with the shootings inside Rooms 120 and 121 and the motel office, the cops would hopefully never figure out. Could be related, could not. Jerry hoped that eventually, the cops would stop caring.

"C'mon," Jerry said to Jade and Holly standing behind him. The sound of sirens in the distance, whether related or not, cinched it. "Let's go. But don't run. Just act like nothing happened."

They made a brisk walk to the two cars. Jade was first to drive out of the parking lot in the Rogue, followed by Jerry and Holly in the rental. As they headed west onto Southwestern Boulevard, they saw two police cars speeding the other way with their lights flashing and sirens blaring.

After a time, Holly reached over and clutched Jerry's forearm. He glanced over at her. But then he looked forward, making sure he could still see Jade.

"What should I do now, Jerry?" Holly asked.

"Go home to your family," Jerry said. "Start over. This has given you a second chance."

"What about a second chance for us?"

He looked at her and shook his head.

"We had our second chance. And our third and our

fourth." He sighed. "We've run out of chances."

"What about this morning?"

"That shouldn't have happened," he said and glanced at her, then forward again. "And it will never happen again."

After a time, she nodded and whispered, "I know." She let some time pass before asking, "You think they'll ever figure out what really happened back there?"

After considering that a moment, Jerry laughed and said, "I can't figure it out. How can they?"

Chapter Forty-Seven
Fox's Story

Two hours later, Dan Miller called Jack Fox and told him that he was at the Stadium Inn, the scene of a quadruple murder, with an army of local detectives, state police investigators, county sheriff deputies, and forensics experts. The dead were the motel owner, Hussein Mohammed Abdullah, found on the floor behind the counter in the motel office; Jeff Flaherty—yes, *the* Jeff Flaherty, with half his face blown off, sprawled on the bloody carpet inside Room 120, just on the other side of the open connecting door to Room 121; and, on the floor next to the bed in Room 121, Pete Sharkey and Chuck Bruno with shots to the head. Some of the investigators at the scene, as well as his station commander, had questions for Miller—like what was he doing at the motel with a SORT team ready to conduct a raid of Room 121 an hour or so before the shootings? So far, Miller couldn't provide a good answer.

"Want to fill me in on the details now, Jack?" Miller asked. "Like why you sent me on what appears to be a wild goose chase to this frigging motel? What the fuck was supposed to go down in Room 121 tonight that didn't, but ended up as a quadruple murder instead?"

Jerry had already called Fox and filled him in on what exactly had gone down. He also assured Fox that he and Jade and Holly had safely returned to the room at the Holiday Inn across from the airport. Of course, Fox couldn't tell Miller that story.

"You can start by telling me who was the bait in Room 121, the guy Sharkey was going to kidnap?" Miller persisted.

"Jeff Flaherty," Fox lied.

"Jeff Flaherty? How's that?"

"Well, it's kinda complicated," Fox said. "So bear with me." He sighed, trying to get his story straight so that it would at least sound reasonable enough to satisfy Miller and stop his further inquiry.

"Flaherty was being set up by Pete Sharkey," Fox began. "See, I found out through Chuck Bruno. He's an investigator with Global, or used to be. He found out that Flaherty had hired Sharkey to help find a place to stash the Global money in some overseas account. This was another of Sharkey's specialties in addition to finding missing persons and fugitives—money-laundering. Sharkey told Flaherty he'd look into it. Of course, when Sharkey was hired to do this, Flaherty didn't give him the account where the million dollars was stashed. That would only happen once Sharkey gave them a good overseas account to ship the stolen money into. Sharkey would receive a twenty percent finder's fee."

"Okay," Miller mumbled dubiously.

"Anyway," Fox went on, "Bruno was following Jeff Flaherty and Holly Shaw around for Global and saw them meet up with Sharkey. At some point, he broke into their apartment in Lackawanna and planted a recording device, and that's how he learned what Sharkey was doing for them." Fox stopped a moment and asked, "You still getting this, Dan?"

After a moment, Miller said, "Yeah, I—I think so. What kind of recording device?"

"A Q-bug," Fox said. He lifted and examined it in between the index and forefinger of his right hand, the small, square device, smaller than a postage stamp, that Bruno had planted on the curtain in his hospital room three mornings ago.

"Q-bug," Miller said and nodded. "So Chuck Bruno learned of the deal between Sharkey and Flaherty and Missus Shaw. Find an overseas account to put Flaherty's Global money into, for a twenty-percent finder's fee."

"Right."

"Okay. Go on."

"Well, it appears that Bruno decided to use this information to take Flaherty and Sharkey down in one fell swoop. First, he went to Flaherty and told him he knew all about his deal with Sharkey. Then, he somehow convinced Flaherty that he couldn't trust Sharkey; that Sharkey would kill him for sure once he gave him the account where the Global money was stashed; and, that he, Bruno could do the same thing—find him an account to launder the Global money. And while Sharkey was charging him a twenty-percent fee, Bruno would charge him only ten. Plus, of course, he wouldn't be dead after giving Bruno temporary control of the money.

"Finally, Bruno convinced Flaherty to get out of his

apartment and get a room at some motel and hide out from Sharkey until arrangements could be finalized for the transfer of the Global money. The following night, at nine o'clock, Bruno would show up, and they'd make the exchange." Fox paused a moment and asked, "You still getting this, Dan?"

"Sort of."

"Well, keep listening," Fox said. "It gets clearer. Flaherty made a deal with Bruno, double-crossing Sharkey in the process, and ended up in Room 121 at the Stadium Inn. Then, Bruno went to see Sharkey, and told him about his deal with Flaherty, but that he didn't want to be partners with that scumbag. He'd rather be partners with Sharkey, and they could split the money fifty-fifty. All Sharkey had to do was break into Flaherty's room at nine o'clock, and make him give them the account where the Global money was stashed and after forcing it out of him, kill Flaherty."

"So how...?"

"I'm getting to that," Fox went on. "See, Chuck Bruno had concocted a fake double-double cross."

"A what?"

"A fake double-double-cross," Fox said and smiled, thinking of the real one Jerry had pulled. A fake quadruple double-cross actually. "After convincing Flaherty to take Room 121, and Sharkey to break into it at nine last night, Bruno came to see me. He knew I had contacts with the local police that he didn't. He'd found the perfect way to set up both Jeff Flaherty and Pete Sharkey in one fell swoop, and get Global's one million dollars back. That would make him the star of the Global's Fraud Unit, and a shoo-in to get the old Chief's job once the chief retired, not to mention a hefty bonus for engineering the whole thing. At least, that's what he told me, and that's what I figured. It made perfect sense.

"So," Fox went on, "that's when I called you and set up the sting. Only Bruno had a better idea than becoming Chief of the Global's Fraud Unit. A setup in which he could land half a million dollars and still keep his job and that involved a double-cross of me."

"Now, I'm lost," Miller said.

"No, it's easy," Fox said. "See, he was working with Sharkey all along. While you and your SORT team were waiting outside of Room 121, Bruno and Sharkey were waiting inside Room 120; and, when you and your boys left, at around 9:30, they sprang into action. They broke into Room 121 using the connecting door and then… something went horribly wrong. Flaherty must have had a gun, and in the fire fight that followed—the logistics of which even I can't figure out—there were three dead bodies left lying on the carpets of Rooms 120 and 121."

After another few moments, Miller asked, "What about the Arab owner of the motel, Abdullah or whatever? Why was he killed? How does he figure into all this?"

Fox wasn't too happy that an innocent bystander had been killed. But that was on Jeff Flaherty, and with Flaherty's death, justice had been served.

"I have no idea," Fox lied. "Maybe it's unrelated. A robbery gone bad. A disgruntled motel guest. Someone who doesn't like Muslims."

Ballistics tests would later confirm that the bullet fired from the stolen pistol found on the carpet in Room 121 that had killed Pete Sharkey matched the bullet that had killed the Muslim owner of the Stadium Inn. Thus, the same stolen pistol had been used in both killings demonstrating that they weren't unrelated as Fox had surmised. When Miller called three weeks later and gave Fox that new bit of news, Fox played dumb and told Miller that he still couldn't any make sense of it either.

"What about the girl?"

"What girl?" Fox asked, playing dumb, almost forgetting about Jade's unexpected appearance at Room 121 just short of nine o'clock.

"She looked a lot like Holly Shaw," Miller added.

"You mentioned she was a blonde, the girl you saw," Fox said.

"Yes, she was. Blonde."

"Well, didn't Holly change into a brunette after she went to prison?" Fox asked.

Miller said, "Yeah, I think you're right. So who was she, the girl I saw."

"I have no idea," Fox lied. "An escort, maybe?"

"In the middle of all that, Flaherty hires an escort?"

"I told you," Fox said. "I don't have all the answers to this puzzle. You asked who Sharkey's kidnapping victim was, and I told you, Jeff Flaherty. The rest of it, you'll have to figure out." He laughed and added, "That's why you state police fellows get paid the big bucks."

Miller scoffed at that and got quiet. After a sigh, he said, "Figure it out? I doubt we'll ever do that."

Finally, Miller asked, "So why couldn't you tell me any of this when you called me to set up the sting—that Flaherty was the bait and what it was about?"

"Chuck Bruno asked me not to," Fox said. "Though, to be honest, his reasons for not wanting you to know before the sting went down were unclear. But now we know the reason why. He and Sharkey were involved together, and were double-crossing not only Flaherty but you and me."

Fox said nothing else. There was no way to make a lie make sense. He'd gone far enough, and he felt terrible anyway for having to take advantage of such a good cop like Dan Miller. But he had no other choice. To tell him the truth would require him to give up the Anonymous Man. And he wasn't about to do that.

Chapter Forty-Eight
Jade's Threat

For the first time in a week, ever since he'd found out that Jeff and Holly had been let out of prison, Jerry got a good night's sleep. He had slept with Jade in one of the two beds in the hotel room while Holly took the other—the one in which he'd had sex with her earlier that day. When Jerry woke up just after eight, he turned to Jade, who was also up, and whispered, "I finally slept."

"I didn't," she said. She nodded across the room at Holly who appeared to be still asleep on her bed. "I had one eye open on her."

"You didn't need to," Jerry suggested, "Without Jeff, she's not bad."

That comment seemed to bother Jade. She gave him a long, cold look. Finally, she said, "You fucked her yesterday, didn't you?"

The question took Jerry by surprise, but he wasn't surprised that Jade had, by her womanly intuition, guessed the truth. He regretted betraying her yesterday, and would forever regret it. He'd acted like a stupid, silly boy. He wanted to tell Jade he couldn't help himself. Fucking Holly was getting back at Jeff, not her. That was the best explanation he could have offered. The other one would only hurt and likely end their relationship. He still had feelings for Holly despite everything that had happened between them the last five years, and despite all the bad things she had done to him.

Instead of that, Jerry lied. "No, I didn't," he whispered, deciding in the end that a lie was better than the truth that would wreck them.

"You're fucking asshole," Jade hissed. "And you're full of shit." She turned her back to him, and Jerry could tell she was sobbing. He tried rubbing her naked shoulders, but she jerked away.

"You still my front?" he whispered into her ear, pleading.

After a time, she whispered, "Yes."

He held her and turned her to him, and they kissed. The lie had worked, or she was pretending to believe him; and, Jerry vowed that it would be the last lie he'd ever tell her.

After a time, they heard Holly stirring from the other bed. She yawned and after stretching out her arms, asked, "What time is it?"

Jerry checked the digital read on the alarm clock. "Eight-fifteen." He twisted around and looked at her. She'd slept in her clothes, and her brown hair was mussed and in disarray. Still, she looked pretty and too much like Jade.

"Time to get up," Jerry added. "Jade and I need to split."

"Get back to your son," Holly said. Her voice expressed

sadness and Jerry wondered if it had something to do with the fact that she had never given him a son.

Holly had called her brother Raymond the night before and told him she'd need a place to stay for a while until she could get on her feet. He was glad to hear that she had finally extricated herself from Jeff. Later, watching the eleven o'clock news, he'd find out why. He called Holly after the report and asked if she knew what had happened. She lied that she didn't. Jeff had gone out last night and didn't tell her where he was going or why. Why he ended up dead, she had no idea. She only knew that Jeff must have gotten himself in some kind of trouble but it didn't involve her. A week later, Dan Miller would come to question Holly, and she'd tell them the same thing. The night Jeff had been killed, she'd been in her apartment when Jeff had gone out, not telling her where he was going. She had no idea, no insight, into his killing that night.

They quickly showered and dressed, and while waiting for Jerry to check them out of the hotel, Jade called Faith. Little Seius was fine, drinking his formula, sleeping okay.

Jade followed with Holly in the Rogue while Jerry returned the rental to a place on Genesee Street across from the airport not far from the hotel. During the ride over, Jade told Holly that if she ever contacted Jerry again, she'd kill her.

Chapter Forty-Nine
Holly's Penance

After dropping off the rental car, Jerry took Jade and Holly to a McDonald's for a quick breakfast. It was almost ten, and Jerry lamented, so much for the early start. No matter what, they were leaving for Florida that day, taking the usual twenty-hour or so ride down south. Hopefully, by nine or ten that night, they'd make it to Wytheville, Virginia. Tomorrow, they'd get an early start and get to see their baby boy sometime that evening.

Jerry, Jade, and Holly didn't talk much as they munched their breakfast sandwiches, hash browns and washed it down with strong cups of coffee. Each seemed wrapped in their thoughts, tired after all they'd been through the last few days and especially, the night before. Some part of each of them was in shock. For Jerry, there was relief as well. Jeff was out of his life for good, and soon Holly would be, and to his surprise, he was still the Anonymous Man.

After McDonald's, Jerry drove to a quiet, middle-class neighborhood in Williamsville, a northern suburb of Buffalo. Holly's brother, Raymond, lived in a four-bedroom red-brick colonial with his pretty wife, Sarah, and two pre-teen girls, about halfway down Garner Road, a tree-lined street among other spacious three- and four-bedroom brick colonials with well-kept lawns and decks in long backyards. Some of the homes, like Raymond's, also had an inground pool in the backyard.

Jerry pulled onto Garner Road and quickly parked along the curb in front of the second house from the intersection with the always busy Sheridan Drive. He recalled Raymond's house being seven down on the other side of the street. He stared at it, remembering the many times in their seven years of marriage when he and Holly had visited for birthday parties, Christmas and other holidays, and backyard barbecues. Holly especially had liked to go there in the summer to go swimming and show off her tan, slender body in a skimpy bikini.

After a time, Jerry looked back at Holly who sat with a tired, woeful expression in the backseat.

"Well, here we are," Jerry said. "I can't exactly pull into his driveway and say hello."

Holly gave half a smile and said to Jerry, "I know. You're dead."

When Holly sat there for a time, seemingly unable to move, Jade let out an exasperated gasp. In the next moment, she exited the front passenger seat and opened the back door.

"Time to go, Holly," Jade said. "Start a new life."

With a glance forward at Jerry, Holly said, "Thanks, Jerry. For giving me another chance." Jerry turned and nodded back at her, still wondering if this was the right thing to do. But what other choice did he have? There was nothing to tie her to the quadruple killings back at the Stadium Inn, though she could certainly shed some light on what had happened. But if she did that, she'd have to give him up and the Anonymous Man as well.

"You're welcome, Hol," he said. "Just take advantage of it."

"I promise, I will."

"Come on Holly," Jade said from outside the rear door. "Let's get this over with."

Finally, Holly slid out of the backseat and exited the car. She stood there for a moment, inches from Jade. A car drove past, and the driver gave the two women standing there a second look. Jerry noticed, and thought the driver must be admiring their good looks and how much they resembled each other.

Jade leaned forward and whispered into Holly's ear, "Remember what I told you, bitch, I'll kill you."

Holly smirked and watched as Jade stepped away from her, turned, and smiling, got back into the passenger seat and slammed the door. Jerry put the car in gear and drove off. He turned around in a driveway on the other side of the street and drove back toward the intersection with Sheridan Drive. As he drove past Holly, she lifted her right hand and gave a half-hearted wave.

Jerry didn't wave back.

After they made a right turn onto Sheridan, he asked Jade, "What did you tell her back there?"

"I wished her good luck," Jade lied, staring forward, clenching her teeth.

With a frown, Jerry turned to her and Jade looked at him and smiled. After a time, she asked, "Can we get on the road and out of this crappy city? Go back to some decent weather?"

"No, not quite," Jerry said. "We have one last stop to make."

Chapter Fifty
One Last Stop

Late that morning, Dick Reynolds, the grizzled, white-haired Chief of Global Life and Casualty Insurance's Special Frauds Unit, sat in a wide chair next to Jack Fox's hospital bed. He'd flown in that morning from Philly after hearing the news about Chuck Bruno's death. After spending over an hour at the Orchard Park Police Department headquarters, trying to make sense out of how Bruno had come to be shot and killed, along with Pete Sharkey and Jeff Flaherty, he'd driven to Buffalo General Hospital to see Fox.

"This one really has me stumped, Jack," Reynolds said. "I'm not surprised, though. It's connected to that Jerry Shaw case."

Fox shrugged. He had not expected Reynolds to make the trip to personally review what had happened. But his bosses at Global were dismayed, and a little miffed, that they'd lost an experienced investigator without explanation and nothing to show for it. Adding insult to injury, they'd have to pay a hefty benefit to the widow of one of their own killed in the line of duty. Reynolds was feeling the heat, and getting the jibe that maybe his days were numbered as Chief of the Special Fraud Unit. After all, he had just turned seventy, and his inability to find the rest of the money in the Shaw case had not earned him any favors with the higher-ups.

"I have no idea what happened, Dick," Fox lied. He felt bad about that, but for some reason, he felt more loyal to the Anonymous Man than Global.

Chief Reynolds perhaps suspected something. His intuition was telling him what Inspector Miller suspected—Fox was holding back. He took some time to repeat what Miller had told him about Fox's involvement and mentioned how curious it all was.

Fox shrugged and decided not to act indignant and challenge the Chief's dubious frown. "All I know is what I know, Dick," Fox said. "Bruno was trying to set up Sharkey when something went wrong. Terribly wrong."

Chief Reynolds' frown intensified. After a time, he let out a sigh and stood. He walked to the tall window overlooking the asphalt roof of the building at the far edge of the hospital parking lot.

"Not much of a view from up here," Reynolds groaned. "Goddamn depressing." He turned and faced Fox with his hands behind his back. "When the hell you getting out of here?"

"Tomorrow is the hope," Fox said. "Depends on the X-rays they took this morning."

Reynolds nodded and seemed distracted again. Finally, he said, "Just doesn't make any goddamned sense." He sighed.

"I'm missing something."

A moment later, Jerry and Jade walked into the room holding hands.

Fox looked over, and his eyes got wide. Nodding to Jerry, he said, "Oh, hi, Steven."

Jerry glanced at Reynolds standing at the side of Fox's bed and nodded at him. He turned back to Fox and said, "Hi, Uncle Jack, how you feelin'?"

"Good," Fox answered. "Maybe getting out tomorrow." He looked to Reynolds, then back at Jerry. "Meet my old boss, Chief Dick Reynolds, from Global Insurance. Chief, meet my nephew, Steven. And his fiancé…"

"Andrea," Jerry finished for him.

"Oh, yeah," Fox said with a laugh. "Of course, Andrea. Another senior moment."

Jerry stepped forward and shook Dick Reynolds' hand. "Hello, sir." With a frown, he asked, "So, what brings you to Buffalo, Mister Reynolds? Not my Uncle, I hope."

"Well, not entirely," he said. "Business, too. Seems one of our investigators got himself killed last night. And while I was here, thought I'd stop in and pay my respects to this old coot. Heard that he got himself beat up a few days back."

"Killed, you said?"

"Yes," Fox said. "One of the guys killed at the Stadium Inn last night. You hear about that?"

"Yes, we did," Jade chimed in. "Heard it on the news this morning."

"What happened, Mister Reynolds?" Jerry asked. "The TV report didn't say much."

Fox glared at Jerry as if to say, *quit being cute and get out of here.*

Reynolds shrugged and gave a vacant look. "Hell if I

know," he said. "Everyone's clueless."

Jerry turned to Fox and said, "Well, Uncle Jack, we just stopped in to say hello, see how you were doing."

"I'm doing fine," Fox said. "As I said, I'll soon be getting out of this place, at long last."

"That's great, Uncle," Jerry said. "Jade and I are off on our trip to Disney World."

"Oh, yeah?" Reynolds said. "Haven't been there in years. Ever since the kids grew up."

Jerry nodded at Jade and said, "Ja...Andrea loves Disney."

"Yes, I do."

"But before I go, I wanted to give you something, Uncle," Jerry said.

"Yeah, what?"

"A little present," Jerry said as he stepped forward and put a thin paper bag in Fox's lap.

"What kind of present?"

"Check it out," Jerry said. As Fox picked up the paper bag, Jerry explained, "It's that comic book you like. Issue two of The Anonymous Man."

Fox pulled out the thin comic book and smiled. On the cover was a man in a hoodie, his face a shroud, hidden from view. Fox looked up at Jerry and said, "Why thanks...Steven."

With a smile, Jerry nodded and said, "Thanks, Uncle Jack. My pleasure."

After a moment, Reynolds approached Fox's bed. He plucked the comic out of Fox's hand and started flipping through it.

"What's it, a superhero comic?"

"Yes," Fox said.

"Never heard of this one," Reynolds said. "The

Anonymous Man." He looked at the cover and added, "And look, it's by Anonymous. Clever."

"Well, Uncle Jack," Jerry said, "we have to get going." He looked to Reynolds and with a nod, said, "Nice meeting you Mister Reynolds."

"Same to you."

Jerry grabbed Jade's hand and started walking toward the door, but stopped after a moment.

"Bye, Uncle Jack," he said. "See you in the comics."

Bye Anonymous Man, Fox thought and almost choked up. "Bye, Steven. And be careful out there."

Chapter Fifty-One
The Anonymous Man

At eleven o'clock at night, a month later, after feeding Seius, changing his diaper and putting him down for, hopefully, the night, Jade found Jerry in his drawing room. She sauntered in and yawned by his desk as she looked over his shoulder.

"How's it coming?" she asked and yawned again. "Issue Number Three?"

As he continued sketching the latest storyboard on the pad before him, Jerry shrugged. "It's coming all right. In this scene, Oscar Plato is hot on his trail."

"I forgot to tell you," she said, "Faith called this afternoon while you were out at the bookstore in Posner Park."

Jerry stopped drawing and swiveled to her. She fell into him and yawned again.

"How is she?" he asked. "The apartment okay? Money holding out?"

"She sounded fine," Holly replied. "Apartment's fine, and she had no complaints about money. Didn't ask for any, anyway. She talked mostly about school. How hard the business law online course is and what a stickler her professor is."

Jerry drew Jade to him, kissed her hair and said, "Glad things are working out for her."

"Thanks to the Anonymous Man," she said.

"Seius gave you no trouble tonight?"

"Not as much as he gave you last night," she said, and laughed.

"Yeah," Jerry said. "What a stinker he can be."

"Just like his father," Jade said. "And, speaking of stinkers, I screwed up today at the Publix. I forgot to pick up more diapers. We are completely out."

Jerry sighed and frowned at her. "And you need me to go get some?"

"Unless you want to put up with a very unhappy baby boy crying through the night, yes. The 7-Eleven on 27 is open all night."

Jerry groaned, looked back at his drawing pad and gently pushed Jade back and himself off his swivel chair.

"I'm sorry, Jer," Jade said with a pouty look.

"I know," he said and kissed her cheek. "It'll take twenty minutes, and our happy baby boy is worth that."

On his way out the door, Jade told him to be careful driving.

Ten minutes later, Jerry strolled into the 7-Eleven on a quiet, warm night. There was only one other car parked along the row right up next to the store, and another car at one of the pumps with the driver nowhere to be found.

Inside the store, Jerry quickly found a box of infant-sized

diapers and paid a heavyset, red-haired, pimply teenage clerk working the dreaded graveyard shift. But on his way out of the store, Jerry found trouble. Three Latino kids in their late teens walked into the store with hard expressions. As they walked past Jerry, one of them pulled out a pistol and pointed it at the clerk.

"The fucking money, asshole."

Jerry froze, and in the next moment, another of the Latino teens turned and pointed a pistol at his head.

"Stay right there, gringo," the second kid said to Jerry in a low, gravelly voice. As Jerry adjusted the box of diapers under his right arm and turned slightly toward him, the kid added, "Keep your fucking eyes straight, si? Not on me."

"Si, senor," Jerry whispered.

"What the fuck you doing, Payaso?" said the last of the three Latino kids. He was slight, handsome kid with thick brown hair and bright, round eyes. "I said, no."

The teen pointing the gun at Jerry turned and said, "Shut the fuck up, Gustavo, you pussy."

A thousand thoughts raced through Jerry's head as his heart began racing. If he did nothing but obeyed these punks, was he dead anyway?

"Hurry up, man," the kid at the counter shouted as the store clerk fumbled for whatever was in the cash register. Jerry noticed another customer for the first time, probably the guy whose car was at the pump. He had moved aside from the counter when the kid barged forward aiming his pistol at the clerk.

Hey, man, Chuco," the one named Gustavo shouted to the kid holding the pistol at the store clerk. "I'm not in this, man. I'm not fucking in this. You have to tell me, man, first."

"Shut the fuck up, Gustavo," said the kid holding the pistol at Jerry's head. "You're in this now, faggot."

At that moment, Jerry thought of lunging toward the one holding the pistol on him and grabbing his arm. And then, doing what? Taking his pistol from him somehow and then engaging Chuco in a gunfight? Instead, Jerry stood his ground, hoping the store clerk would quickly lift out and turn over whatever cash was in the register, and the three punks would run out of there and be caught by the police somewhere down US 27.

"I ain't doing this," Gustavo mumbled to himself, though loud enough, and started for the door.

"Where the fuck you going?" Payaso said. "You walk out, you're dead."

"Hurry the fuck up!" the kid at the counter shouted, focused only on the money. Jerry glanced that way and saw that the clerk was finally handing over a wad of cash. But in the next moment, the money fell out of his hands. It splashed onto the counter, and a good portion of it fell onto the floor. Just then, another car pulled into the lot.

The kid at the counter saw it and said, "Fuck."

By then, Gustavo pushed open the door and walked out.

Payaso reached down and grabbed what cash he could and trotted toward the front door. The one aiming the pistol at Jerry quickly joined him. By now, all three of the Latino boys were outside. For a moment, Payaso stood shouting at Gustavo on the sidewalk in front of the store with the other one, Chuco, waving his arms, still holding the pistol, as if admonishing them to get the fuck going. Finally, Jerry winced and ducked when he saw Payaso point his pistol at Gustavo. Gustavo stood there and closed his eyes. Payaso pulled the trigger, but the gun misfired, and there was no time to figure out why.

Payaso ran off with Chuco toward their old compact car with a faded hood, as if it had been in the Florida sun far too long. He shouted back at Gustavo, "You're fucking dead!"

Jerry certainly didn't want to get caught up in a police investigation of the robbery. As the car streaked out of the parking lot, he hurried out of the store. On his way out, he heard the clerk shout after him, "Hey, Mister!"

Outside, Jerry saw Gustavo watch Chuco and Payaso as they sped out of the 7-Eleven lot onto the northbound US 27, probably heading back to Poinciana or Orlando.

"Hey, kid," Jerry said as he approached. "Come with me."

Gustavo turned to him, his bright eyes narrowed into a scowl.

"What?"

"I said come with me," Jerry said. "I'll hide you out for a while, change your life. Get you away from them." Jerry nodded north toward US 27 where the car had gone. Sirens howled from that direction; one or more Polk County Sheriff's cruisers speeding to the rescue.

"You can't stay here," Jerry said. "And neither can I."

Jerry hurried to the driver's side door and clicked the remote to unlock it. As he opened the door, he urged the kid, "C'mon," with a welcoming nod.

After a moment, Gustavo came around to the passenger side and got into Jerry's car.

Jerry started it and as he drove out of the lot, moments before the first of the deputy's cruisers pulled in, Gustavo asked, "Who the hell are you?"

Jerry turned to him with a smile. "The Anonymous Man."

Thank You!

Thank you for reading our book and for supporting stories of fiction in the written form. Please consider leaving a reader review on Amazon and Goodreads, so that others can make an informed reading decision.

Find more exceptional stories, novels, collections, and anthologies on our website at: **digitalfictionpub.com**

Join the **Digital Fiction Pub** newsletter for infrequent updates, new release discounts, and more. Subscribe at: **digitalfictionpub.com/blog/newsletter/**

See all our exciting fantasy, horror, crime, romance and science fiction books, short stories and anthologies on our **Amazon Author Page** at: **amazon.com/author/digitalfiction**

Also from Digital Fiction

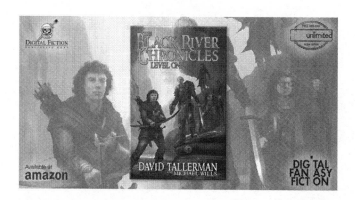

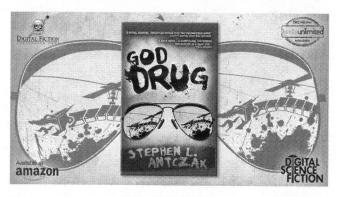

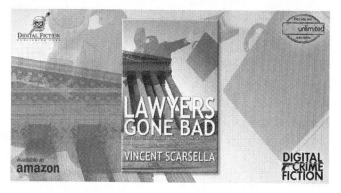

About the Author

 Vincent L. Scarsella is the author of speculative, fantasy, and crime fiction. His published books include the crime novels The Anonymous Man (2013) and Lawyers Gone Bad (2014), as well as the young adult fantasy, Escape from the Psi Academy, Book 1 of the Psi Wars! Series released in May, 2015. Book 2 of the series, Return to the Psi Academy, is slated for publication by IFWG Publishing in the summer of 2016.

Scarsella has also published numerous speculative fiction short stories in print magazines, such as The Leading Edge, Aethlon, and Fictitious Force, various anthologies, and in several online zines. His short story, "The Cards of Unknown Players," was nominated for the Pushcart Prize and has been republished by Digital Science Fiction (an imprint of Digital Fiction Pub).

Scarsella's full-length play, Hate Crime, about race relations in the context of a legal thriller, was performed in Buffalo on September 13, 2016 and is scheduled for a reprise in late May of 2016. The Penitent, about the Catholic Church child molestation scandal, was a finalist in the June 2015 Watermelon One-Act Play Festival.

Scarsella has also published non-fiction works, most notably, The Human Manifesto: A General Plan for Human Survival, which was favorably reviewed in September 2011 by the Ernest Becker Foundation.

Copyright

Still Anonymous
Written by **Vincent L. Scarsella**
Executive Editor: **Michael A. Wills**
Copy Editor: **Kay Nash**